VAMPYR

The Building 4 Series Book II

SHIGERU BRODY

1

The screams were like candy to his ears.

That beautiful sound bounced off the trees and reverberated off the ancient stones as a breeze whispered through the darkened forest. With his vampire eyes, Jerreck Simone could see the girl running through the brush, narrowly missing blue ash trees that towered over her. She slipped and fell once and cut her leg. The blood flowing from her caused his heart to pound.

But there was something different about the screams: he hadn't caused them.

He sat perched on the branch of a tall tree like some monstrous crow, observing the prey below him, waiting for them to die. The girl was young—seventeenish—and pretty. Jerreck took in the scent of her predator—behind the girl, maybe twenty feet.

The young man ran after her with such ferocity that he didn't stop even when he'd clearly injured himself tripping over some rocks. He was grunting like a pig, and Jerreck could see a length of rope and a knife tucked into his waistband.

Out of breath and leaning against the tree, the girl begged for her life. The man stood nearby and didn't speak or move. *He's relishing it*, Jerreck thought.

The man took out the knife. The girl tried to run, but the blade plunged into her belly. She looked up at the man, and their eyes met as her warm blood spilled to the ground.

Jerreck had to look away, taking in deep breaths, telling himself to stay calm. The blood called to him, and he wanted to go there and suck both of the humans dry. But he didn't. That would ruin the fun.

When Jerreck looked back, the man was still stabbing the girl in the chest and stomach. Then he stumbled backward and dropped the knife. Jerreck could smell panic on him.

The young man took off, sprinting through the woods as quickly as he could.

Jerreck glided off the tree, landing silently on the forest floor. He crouched over the woman as she died, took some of her blood on his fingers, and tasted it. The ecstasy of it made him weak.

He watched the young man tear through the woods, heading for a car that was parked in a secluded area near a stream.

What an interesting little boy you are, he thought.

2

In the morning light, few places were as creepy to Hadrian Brams as the middle of the forest. The way the sun broke into splinters through the twisted trees, the multitude of insects crawling over the ground, and trying to get up your leg, not to mention the animals... he wondered why the hell he'd moved to Spirit Lake, Virginia, of all places if he felt that way.

"Deputy Brams," Sheriff Wright yelled. "Over here."

The sheriff projected strength, but underneath that exterior, Hadrian saw a mess of pain and sadness. The pain radiated out of her eyes when she wasn't paying attention, and on a deep, gut-level, he felt sorry for her and couldn't exactly say why.

"What do we have, Sheriff?"

"Single victim, female... I knew her. She was a friend of my daughter's. Amanda Sorin. She's still in high school."

Hadrian stepped nearer to the body. The forensics team on loan from the Richmond Police Department was snapping photos and taking measurements. A lovely young girl lay at his feet. Even in this condition, in this environment, her exquisiteness shone through. Several stab wounds, as many as twenty, adorned her body. Little red slits in the gray flesh. Dried blood everywhere.

Sheriff Wright came up behind him and watched the forensic techs work. "You sure the body wasn't drained of blood?" she asked one of them.

"Yes," the tech said. "I mean she's lost a lot of blood, there's a lot on the ground here. But she wasn't drained."

"Any bite marks?"

"None that I can see now, but you'll have to ask the coroner after the autopsy."

"Bite marks?" Hadrian asked.

She exhaled, wiping her hands on her pants. "You're young, Hadrian. When I was your age, the world looked a lot different than it does now. I just want to rule out certain things."

"Like an animal attack?"

"Yeah, like an animal attack." She seemed to be lost in thought for a moment, but when she finally snapped back, she said, "You worked homicides in Los Angeles, didn't you?"

He'd known this was coming. The moment he'd sought out another law enforcement job, he'd known this day would come.

"Sheriff, I became a deputy out here to get away from all that."

"I know you did. You told me that during the interview. But I've got my hands full with other things right now. You're the best I've got for this."

"You don't know that."

"I have a hunch. Please, Hadrian. I know her. I know her family."

Hadrian exhaled. "Sorry, Sheriff. I can't think like this anymore. If you want to fire me, I understand perfectly. But I can't do it."

She nodded and let out a long sigh. "I'm not going to fire you. But I am disappointed."

"I know," he said and headed back to his cruiser.

After his shift ended, Hadrian changed into jeans and a leather jacket and got into his Mustang. He pulled out of the parking lot and headed to the social services building. He retrieved a box from his trunk and then went inside and placed it on the counter. He'd bought the toys yesterday for the orphans and foster children in Spirit Lake. The small town didn't have many such children, but those few that were here were largely ignored. Back in Los Angeles, he'd dropped off a box of toys every six months. Here, because there were few kids and the cost of living was so much less, his salary allowed him to do it once a month.

"Have a good one," he said to the receptionist.

"You too, Hade, thanks."

He made his way to Antonio's Bar. The only things in his fridge at home were beer and an old box of Arm & Hammer. The restaurant was lit well and smelled like cooking food. A few high school kids were shooting pool, and the tables were packed. The chef knew Hadrian personally—he was there every night—so when he nodded, the chef nodded back, indicating that his meal was on its way.

Hadrian found a booth and sat down. He pulled two packets of sugar out of the container on the table and played with them, the image of a young girl torn apart in a forest scorched in his mind. He had seen so many just like her that one more shouldn't have bothered him. He told himself that it didn't, that he was fine. But when he looked down, he realized that he had opened the sugar packets and spilled them over the table without meaning to.

A young woman with two sodas in her hand stumbled on her way past his table and spilled one of the drinks on him. A cold sensation spread through his lap.

She stopped next to him, her mouth open. "Oh my gosh. I am so sorry."

"It's okay," he said, dabbing his pants with some napkins.

"That was totally my fault. I wasn't paying attention, and I just—"

"Really, it's okay." He put the soaked napkin down and took up another one.

"Let me pay for the dry cleaning."

"Nah, they're just pants. It'll come right out."

She placed the glasses on the table. "Let me at least buy you a soda. I feel terrible."

"I won't say no."

She grinned and held out her hand. "Sayer Bellamy. Um, my friends just call me Sadie."

He took her hand. "Hadrian Brams."

Her brow furrowed, and she just stood there.

"Please," he said, "have a seat."

She sat across from him. "I haven't met you before."

"No, I've only been in town a month."

Her demeanor changed, and she appeared serious, a wrinkle in her forehead. "So, what brings you here?"

"I'm a cop. I thought it'd be nice to be one in a quiet little town. But it's turning out to be just as busy as everywhere else."

"Oh, you're a cop."

"You seem relieved."

"It's nothing. So you work for Kristen's mom then? Sheriff Wright?"

"I do."

She took a sip of one of the sodas, the one that still had some in it. "So where'd you live before Spirit Lake?"

"Los Angeles. I was, ah, a junior detective there."

"What kind of detective?"

"Homicide."

"Sorry. I made you uncomfortable."

"No, no. It's just not something I ever talk about, and it's come up twice today."

"Must have been hard. Seeing everything you saw."

He took a sip of her drink. "Well, that's why I moved here. But it looks like I can't get away from it."

"You're talking about Amanda, aren't you?"

"How'd you know that?"

"It's all over."

"You knew her?"

"Not really. We said hello a few times." She hesitated. "But wickedness eventually gets punished."

He took a long drink. "You think so?"

"I do."

He nodded. Suddenly, he didn't feel very hungry. He took out a wad of bills and laid a twenty on the table before rising. "Well, Sayer Bellamy, it was really nice meeting you."

"You too, Hadrian Brams."

He grinned but left with a dull, heavy ache in his gut and the image of a dead girl that refused to leave him.

3

The next day came quickly, and Hadrian didn't get much sleep. He showered and ate a breakfast of cereal and orange juice before donning his uniform and heading out. His first stop was always the sheriff's office for morning roll call. But that day, dispatch let him know that he was the closest unit to a reported crime in progress.

"This is unit two-three-two, heading out now," he said into his radio.

"Roger that, two-three-two. Single male suspect, possibly armed, neighbors reporting possible domestic in progress."

"Ten-four. ETA no more than five minutes."

He turned his cruiser around and headed to the address that popped up on his laptop screen. Oak Ridge. He was familiar with those homes and that section of the city. The part of Spirit Lake that no one talked about, but that every town had. The part everyone tried to ignore.

Furniture was scattered on the lawns, and the homes were run down. Old cars that no longer ran sat in driveways. He'd been called out here two times the past week, all for drug-related offenses.

When he'd first moved there, he thought marijuana would be the drug of choice in a small, sleepy town like Spirit Lake. But he'd actually come to find that methamphetamine was growing more popular. It was cheap and could be made in a trailer with a couple hundred bucks' worth of supplies. The high lasted five times as long as marijuana as well.

The house at the address he'd been given was peach-colored with brown trim. No one was outside, but he could see a man and woman arguing through the windows. Hadrian stepped out of his car and went to the front door. He could hear the couple through the door, but the voices went silent when he knocked.

"Sheriff's Office. Open up!" he said as he undid the thumb break securing his firearm in its holster. He stepped to the side of the door, his hand on his weapon.

He heard the sound of a bolt being unlocked, and then a woman opened the door only a few inches. She had a black eye. "Yes?"

"You okay?"

"Yes."

"I'd like to speak to your husband."

"He ain't here."

"Ma'am, I know he's here. I saw him through the window. Please have him come to the door."

She hesitated and looked over her shoulder before opening the door. Hadrian pulled out his weapon and held it by his side. He stepped in, and the man was sitting on the couch, acting like he had no idea what was going on. Hadrian put his gun away, and then called it in, requesting another unit and an ambulance for a possible facial injury.

"What's your name, man?"

"Mark. What can I do for you, officer? We weren't doin' nothin'."

"I got a complaint of domestic abuse."

"Nah, man, there ain't no domestic abuse here. We just talkin'."

"Yeah, and where'd she get that shiner?"

The woman held her head low, wouldn't meet his eyes.

"She fell."

"She fell, huh?"

"Yup. She fell."

"You got any weapons on you?"

He placed his arms on the back of the couch as if he were just relaxing on any given morning. "Nope."

"Any in the house?"

"Got a shotgun in the closet. It ain't loaded."

"Any kids?"

Neither of them spoke.

"Are there any kids in this house?"

"No, man. No kids."

"I don't believe you. Stand up."

"I didn't do nothin'."

"Stand up now, or I'll taze you in the face."

He groaned and stood.

"Turn around," Hadrian said. The man did as he was

told, and Hadrian cuffed him. He sat him back on the couch. "Those cuffs are there for my safety. I'm going to search the house, and as long as there's no children here, I'm going to uncuff you and issue you a citation. But if you cooperate, I'm not going to take you to jail. Do you understand?"

The man nodded.

The house was quiet. Hadrian crossed into the kitchen, his firearm held low, his finger outside the trigger guard. He checked a door, and behind it was cans of food stacked on shelves. He saw a table with a bowl of cereal on it, and several empty cans of beer sat on the counter.

Hadrian went into the bedroom. The room had an open window facing the backyard, and he could hear a breeze rustling the leaves of a maple tree. As he turned to go, he heard a cough. It came from the closet.

"Sheriff's Office. Please come out with your hands up."

No reply.

He held up his firearm and slid along the wall. He opened the door and peeked his head in.

A small boy sat on the floor, playing with some old toys. He looked up at Hadrian. His eyes were black, and his face swollen and red.

"Hi," the boy said.

Hadrian put the gun away and knelt down. "Hi. What's your name?"

"David."

"David, my name is Hadrian. I'm here to help you. Who… did someone hit you, David?"

"Yeah."

"Was it your daddy?"

"Yeah. He got mad 'cause I spilled my cereal."

Hadrian had to swallow and look away. The boy's face was so puffy that he was having trouble forming his words. "I'm going to take you to a hospital, okay, David? They're going to give you some medicine and make you all better. Okay?"

"Okay."

He picked the child up and walked into the living room. Sirens wailed outside, and he saw the ambulance pull up. Hadrian went out to the porch and handed the child to the paramedics. He watched as they took him into the back of the ambulance. Another sheriff's deputy, Sandy Clarkson, arrived as well. Before she got out of the car, Hadrian went back inside.

He picked the father up by the neck and cocked back his fist. "He's just a kid!" he shouted.

"Don't hurt him!" the mother yelled. She ran to the man's side and covered him with her body.

Hadrian watched them for a moment and then let go. He went outside. Deputy Clarkson was walking up the steps.

"Hey," she said. "What happened?"

"Arrest him for felony child abuse and her too. She let it happen."

Clarkson said something to him, but he didn't hear. He stormed to his cruiser and got in. He saw Clarkson go inside as another deputy came to a stop behind him. Hadrian punched the steering wheel.

He started the car and pulled away.

4

Remy Simone stood in the parking lot of Spirit Lake High School, his backpack slung over one shoulder. Since getting back to town, he'd made it a ritual to come to class even though they had nothing to teach him. After a hundred and sixty-eight years of life, facts were packed so tightly in his head, he felt like he might explode.

He twirled the black and silver medallion in his pocket, the medallion that allowed him to walk in sunlight. Without it, his skin would fry and soon afterward, his organs. He'd even seen vampires whose blood literally boiled inside of them. They bubbled until their skin burst open, and they turned to a goopy puddle.

As he walked inside, he glanced around quickly for his brother Jerreck. He'd shown up at the school once just to antagonize Remy, and he'd never felt secure since.

The halls were filled with students running to class

or loitering by their lockers. His education at their age had consisted of nothing but tutors, so he'd never had the real high school experience. He'd thought maybe he could have it in Spirit Lake, but it turned out he was wrong. No matter how many people he got to know, he always felt like the conductor of an experiment observing his subjects from the outside.

All except her.

He watched as Jordan Lynn walked across the hall to her locker. She was speaking with her little brother about something, and he got angry and stormed off. She placed her hand against her locker and stood there a moment with her eyes closed.

He wanted to run to her. To put his arms around her and tell her that everything was going to be okay. That he would protect her from anything. But he couldn't. Not yet. She only knew him as the new kid that she had agreed to go on a few dates with. Eventually, he would reveal everything about himself. But until then, he had to take it slow.

Remy turned away and headed to his own locker. Down the hall was a locker with a photo of a girl taped to it. Several candles had been placed before it.

Jordan's brother, Thomas, was walking by the other way, apparently heading for the door.

"Hey," Remy said.

"Hey."

"What's this about?" He gestured to the locker and candles.

"Oh, that's Amanda's." Remy shrugged. "Oh, yeah, you're new here, huh? Not enough time to get connected to the grapevine."

"Just been here a little while."

"Amanda was killed a few days ago."

Remy's stomach dropped. "What happened?"

"I don't know the details. Just killed in the woods, I guess."

Remy tried not to appear upset. "Do they know who did it?"

"I don't know, man. I try not to think about that stuff."

Remy watched as Thomas walked out the doors and headed across the parking lot. He stood a moment quietly and then did the same.

Their home was really a mansion and had been used once, long ago, as a boarding house. These days Rich and Remy lived there by themselves, with Jerreck as a somewhat unwanted guest. Though he was glad for Rich—the house could get messy sometimes—he wished his brother would just leave.

Jerreck was sitting on the couch when he walked in, reading a book.

"How goes it, brother?" Jerreck said.

In a flash, Remy had him by the throat and was trying to lift him. Jerreck spun him around and threw him on the couch, his own hand on Remy's throat. Remy refused to drink the human blood that gave a vampire his strength. Jerreck didn't have that hang-up.

"I don't appreciate that," Jerreck said. "It makes me think I'm not welcome in my own house."

"Why'd you kill her?"

"You're going to have to be more specific. I've killed

a lot of people."

"Amanda. The girl from the high school. You killed her three days ago and left her body in the woods."

"Oh, her."

"Yeah," Remy said, slapping away his hand. "Her."

"I was planning on killing her, I was, but someone actually beat me to it."

"Beat you to it?"

"That's what I said."

"You expect me to believe someone else killed your prey the night you just happened to be out hunting?"

"I don't care what you believe, but that's what happened."

Remy held his gaze. "Okay, let's pretend for a moment you're telling the truth. Who was it?"

"I don't know. Never seen him before. Young guy, though. Probably goes to the same high school."

"If I find out you're lying and you actually killed her, I'll—"

"You'll what? Try and take me down with another pro wrestling move?" Jerreck rolled his eyes. "You can't harm me, brother. Not unless you want to start snacking on some Virginians, of course."

"How can you be so casual about it? These are people, Jerreck."

"These people are our food, *Remy*. You used to know that."

Jerreck walked away, leaving Remy staring at his back.

5

Hadrian filled out a ticket for speeding. He sat in his car and ran the guy's name just in case he had any warrants: Abe Wood. Seventeen years old, no warrants, no criminal history. He walked back to the 2015 Tesla Model S, a beautiful car that he had to pause and stare at for a moment.

"Hey man, can't you just let this slide? I swear I just wasn't paying attention."

Hadrian held the ticket a moment and then tore it in half. He wasn't there to be the city's fundraiser. "One warning only. No more speeding."

"No more, I promise. Thanks."

Hadrian walked back to the cruiser and went to reset the ladar gun but stopped. This wasn't why he had become a police officer. Then again, it was mindless and easy. Maybe it was just what he needed? He took out a bag of peanuts, opened it, and shoved a few in his mouth before resetting the ladar gun. His transceiver buzzed.

"Hadrian, you there?" It was Sheriff Wright.

"I'm here, Sheriff."

"I'm at the Olsen's barn, just behind it. Near the Franks' warehouse. You know where it is?"

"Yeah."

"Please get down here right away."

"What is it?"

"I'll explain in person."

Unusual enough for the sheriff to contact him over the transceiver and more so to invite him somewhere without giving him all the details.

Driving down to the Olsen's farm, he listened to Guns N' Roses but kept it turned low. The farm was set near the woods, and the barn, an old red-and-white built near the time of the town's founding, sat at the back of the property hidden away by a thicket of trees.

Several cars and a black van with the words RICH-MOND CRIME SCENE UNIT on the side were already there. He parked but didn't get out. Not for a while. Finally, he turned off the iPhone connected to the stereo, got out, and walked to the barn.

Yellow police tape was set around a body. Sheriff Wright was there with another deputy and the crime scene unit. Hadrian stood frozen until Sheriff Wright saw him and walked over.

"Thanks for coming," she said.

"Who is she?"

"Rebecca Nelson. Seventeen. Goes... went to the same school as Amanda. That's two of them, Hadrian. But the forensics guys are telling me this one was first. They think she's been here at least three weeks. Her mom had put in a missing persons report for her then, but we had a witness that said she ran off with her boyfriend the last time anyone saw her. We didn't treat it like we should have."

"Do you have the boyfriend in custody?" He couldn't keep from staring at the corpse lying in the grass.

"Not yet, but we will." She glanced at the body and then back to Hadrian. "I don't have any experience in… this. I can call Richmond Homicide, but last time I did that, they offered advice and the use of their labs. They don't want to put in work on something that isn't going to get them any credit."

"I…"

"She's seventeen, Hadrian. And she went through hell. She's just a kid."

He swallowed. "I… need a minute."

She nodded. "Sure."

Hadrian left the scene and sat in his car. The girl hadn't even been out of high school. She would never marry, never have children, never experience the comforts of old age. The wisdom that comes with time and the warm regret at how ridiculous she'd been as a child. She wouldn't experience anything anymore. He wasn't technically here for this: he was placed in this town, in this job, to investigate something else. Something ancient and evil… but if he could help stop these killings, how could he say no?

An image came to him of a little girl, dead in a canal, surrounded by graffiti. His first homicide case. He pushed it out of his mind and went back to the sheriff.

"You got me, Liz. I'll find him."

6

Lucian Cody left calculus class and sat on the lawn of the school. Some of the football players were walking out onto the field for practice, followed by the cheerleaders. His eyes never left the girls, and a couple of them smiled at him. He knew he was considered attractive, but he never moved on it. He'd never had a girlfriend or even a conversation with a girl on the phone.

Pulling out some chips and a soda from his backpack, he pretended to watch the players practicing. Just another young sophomore who hoped to try out for the team. But he was really watching the girls.

They varied in hair and skin color, but their figures were all the same and pleasant to look at. At the end of the line they had formed was a young girl he'd come to know quite well. Tammy Fell. Her legs appeared smooth, almost shiny, in the sunlight, and her golden hair came down in curls on her shoulders.

She noticed him observing and smiled. He looked

away, embarrassment burning his face. He lifted his backpack and left.

The walk home wasn't too far, no more than a couple of miles, and the weather was pleasant. The winters were harsh in Spirit Lake, but the summers were relatively cool and the spring and fall perfect.

The sidewalks were empty, and he watched the leaves dance on the ground, kicked by a breeze.

His home was in Oak Ridge. Though no one ever said it—Spirit Lake was such a polite place—that was the poor part of town. Some of the girls at school wouldn't even talk to you if you lived there.

His house was set far back on two-acres of land. The front of the property was all cypress trees and ferns. He unlocked the gate and then locked it again as he walked the path leading to the house.

He sat on the porch steps for a few minutes, not ready to go in, the appearance of Tammy's smile still fresh in his mind.

The window opened behind him.

"Boy, is that you?"

"Yes, Ma."

"Get in here. I need my soup."

He rose and went inside. The house was cluttered but not dirty. His Ma liked to hoard things and could never bring herself to throw anything away, but she also hated germs. This led to stacks of freshly cleaned magazines, books, clothing, twenty-year-old alarm clocks... everything she had ever owned since she was old enough to walk. His room was the only normal one in the house.

Lucian went to the kitchen and fixed his mother some soup. He stood over the stove to cook, and when the soup was done, he lifted the pot to pour it into a bowl. When he turned around, he gasped and dropped the pot.

Before him stood a man in black with gleaming blue eyes. He smiled and looked down at the soup.

"Ma's gonna be pissed," the man said.

"Who are you? How'd you get in here?"

"My name is Jerreck Simone. And you, my clumsy little friend, have piqued my interest. No one's piqued my interest for a long, long time."

"I'm calling the police," Lucian said, going for a phone on the wall.

"No problem. And after you tell them about me, I can talk to them about that night in the forest. The one where you made Swiss cheese out of little Amanda Sorin. And by the way, your ma invited me in. I didn't have to break in."

Lucian froze, staring at the phone. Then he turned around slowly and saw the man smiling, his eyes widening and narrowing randomly. "Who are you?"

"Just someone who finds the strange interesting."

"Are you gonna turn me in?"

"If I wanted to do that, I would have done it. No, I have something much more fun planned."

"What's that?"

"I'm going to help you."

7

Hadrian crouched over the body of Rebecca Nelson. He took a toothpick from his pocket and placed it between his teeth, something he hadn't done over a body for several years.

The girl was lying on her back, her eyes open. Stab wounds covered her torso, and a particularly brutal one was on her throat. He counted at least thirty wounds, more than on Amanda. She had probably died after the first five or six blows. Pure rage. That was the only thing that could get a man to keep stabbing someone after they were already dead.

Forensics was taking photos, and Hadrian snapped on some latex gloves. Carefully, he searched the girl's pockets. The only thing he found was a receipt to Antonio's. Seven dollars for a hamburger and fries.

"Anything?" Sheriff Wright said from behind him.

"Receipt to the Grill. Nothing else in her pockets. Did you guys find a purse laying around?"

"We searched everywhere within five hundred feet. Nothing."

"Get some deputies to search in a circle of a couple thousand feet. He might've dropped something if he ran from here."

"Why would you think he ran?"

"He's inexperienced. These wounds are frantic, just like on Amanda. He doesn't know what he's doing. Some of them hit bone, some of them didn't do anything but cut her clothing. He did this quickly. He's new to this." Hadrian stood. "But he's got a taste for it now. Two vics within three weeks of each other is extremely quick. These types of killers work in cycles, and the cycles are usually months, not weeks. At the beginning, anyway."

She stared at the body. "I got a call they picked up her boyfriend. He's at the station right now."

"I'll go talk to him."

Hadrian drove down to the station quickly. That familiar gnawing sensation in his gut was back. Something he hadn't felt for a long time. Something between anxiety and elation.

He parked and went inside the station. As he was going in, Sayer Bellamy was coming out, accompanied by a blonde.

"Hey," she said with a smile.

"Hey, Sayer. How are you?"

She blushed. "Good."

"What're you doing here?"

"Just picking up Stephanie. Oh, Steph, this is Hadrian."

"Hadrian?" said Stephanie. "I like that name."

"Thanks. It was my grandfather's. Well, I got some

things I have to do. Have a good one, Sayer."

"You too."

They walked off, and Hadrian saw Sayer look back at him. Cute girl, but only seventeen. That was a shame because he hadn't met many women since moving there.

He went inside the station. It seemed like a slow day, and a couple of deputies were standing around the coffee maker gossiping. They said hello, and he nodded as he went back to the interview room.

A deputy was posted outside, and at a table in the room sat a young man with curly hair and a tattoo on his forearm.

"That the boyfriend?" Hadrian asked.

"Yup. Isaac Phillips. All yours."

"Hey, do me a favor and make sure the video's recording, huh?"

"Sure thing."

Hadrian grabbed a soda out of the machine and then came back to the room. He shut the door behind him and placed the soda in front of Isaac.

"What am I doing here?"

"We just had some questions."

"And you couldn't make a call?"

"It's better to do things in person. People tend to be more truthful with you when you can look them in the eyes."

He leaned back. "I got nothin' to hide."

"Really? Your girlfriend is missing for three weeks, and you don't call us or offer to help in any way?"

"What can I do, man? I'm just a mechanic. I ain't a

cop. And where the hell is she?"

"Rebecca?"

"Yeah, Rebecca. That's why I'm here, right? So, where is she? I wanna talk to her."

"So you're telling me you don't know that she's dead?"

A long silence. "She's dead?"

"Stabbed over thirty times. You didn't know?"

"Why the hell would I know?"

Hadrian considered him. The shock on his face was genuine. "She had a receipt from Antonio's in her pocket from three weeks ago, May twenty around eight o'clock. Were you with her that night?"

"I don't know. What day is that?"

"It's a Thursday."

He ran his hand through his hair. "No, Thursdays I work until nine, and then I go to the gym. Check with the gym if you don't believe me. I'm there, like, five nights a week."

"I will." Hadrian leaned back in his seat. "When her mother reported her missing, someone told us she ran off with you."

"Yeah, man. She came over to my house and crashed sometimes. Her mom's a boozer, and when she's drunk, she's an asshole."

"Do you know anyone that wanted to hurt Rebecca?"

"No."

Hadrian watched as Isaac reached for the soda, opened it, but didn't take a sip. "How old are you, Isaac?"

"Twenty-one."

"What're you doing messing around with high school girls?"

He placed his hands on the table, his fingers interlaced. "Hey, we never had sex. There's no rule against dating."

Hadrian nodded. "I may have some more questions for you. Don't leave town for a while."

"Got nowhere to go. Can I leave now? I'm missing work."

"Yeah, you can go."

Hadrian didn't move for a few minutes. His gut told him Isaac didn't have anything to do with Rebecca's murder, but then again, his gut had been wrong before. He called the gym, and the front desk clerk searched the computer for check-in times for Isaac.

"Yup," the clerk said. "May twentieth, he was here from nine sixteen to twenty past ten."

"Thanks."

The times didn't add up. Didn't completely rule him out as the time of death could be off. Still, it certainly didn't help, considering the coroner said Rebecca likely was killed between five and nine. That would place Isaac at work and then the gym. He wouldn't have had an opportunity to do it.

Hadrian rose and left the room, glancing up to the camera in the corner as he went.

<h1 style="text-align:center">8</h1>

Antonio's Bar & Grill was packed with the night crowd. The bar was congested, the tables were full, and even more people were out on the patio.

Lucian sat at a table by himself and ate steak. He had enjoyed people-watching since he was a kid, and his mother had routinely left him on a bench, done her shopping, and picked him up several hours later.

People fascinated him. That one person could actually care what happened to another was so alien to Lucian, that they may as well have been able to fly. It would have perplexed him just about as much.

A girl walked in, and his heart dropped. Jordan Lynn. She was with the new boy that all the girls were talking about, Remy Simone. He was ridiculously good-looking, and a wave of insecurity and jealousy went through Lucian. Even though, according to some of the girls he'd eavesdropped on in the locker room, he was just as good-looking.

But that's not what he saw when he looked in the

mirror. What he saw was a scar. One giant, walking, talking scar. He didn't understand why anyone placed any value on him. And those were just the scars he couldn't see. The physical scar, the one he could see, was a gift from his father and ran down from his eye to his chin. A constant reminder of where he had come from.

He finished the steak and gulped down the rest of his soda. Even though he wasn't hungry anymore, he still ordered dessert so he could watch Jordan a little longer. The way her hair came down and tickled her shoulders, her deep brown eyes with a sparkle of curiosity and intelligence and, most of all, pain. She'd lost her parents a little while ago. Lucian had lost his parents, too. The woman he called mother was really his grandmother. Other than her, he had no family.

He walked to their table and then stood staring down at her. She looked up, and his heart fluttered. The words he wanted to say wouldn't come out.

Remy said, "You okay?"

Lucian opened his mouth, but to his horror, no words came. So he turned and left without looking back.

Once outside, he sucked in breath, leaning against the wall.

"Stupid, stupid," he mumbled to himself. As he walked away, heading home, a shadow appeared in front of him.

"Hello, Lucian."

Startled, he took a step back. Out of the darkness, Jerreck Simone walked toward him with a smile.

"What do you want?" Lucian stammered.

"I want to help you. I told you that."

"Help me what?"

"You know…" He slid his finger across his throat and made a choking sound.

"I don't know what you're talking about."

"Again? I thought we were past this?"

"I… it was an accident. I didn't mean to do it."

"Really? Because I was right there, and it didn't look like your knife just accidentally fell into her a dozen times."

"How were you right there? There wasn't anybody there."

"Oh, I can be quite subtle when I want to be." Jerreck stepped close to him. "Let me ask you something, and answer me honestly because I can tell when you're lying. Why'd you kill her?"

Lucian hesitated. "I don't know."

"I told you to be honest."

"I am being honest. For as long as I can remember, I've wanted to kill someone. I don't know why. Something's wrong with me. With my brain. I don't know why I did it."

"How did it feel?"

He swallowed. "It felt good."

"Was she the first?"

Silence.

"Oh, she wasn't the first. You surprise me, little leprechaun."

"Are you going to turn me in?"

"No."

"Why not? Anybody else would."

"I'm not anybody else." He placed his arm around Lucian's shoulders as they began to walk. "See, Lucian, you"—he tapped the boy's nose with one finger—"are very beautiful to me. And I like to keep beautiful things around."

9

The lighting in the gym was harsh fluorescence, and Hadrian had complained once to the owner that it gave headaches to people sensitive to their environments. But the owner basically said the gym was just a tax deduction, and he didn't plan on spending any more money on it.

Hadrian lifted weights to exhaustion, got some water, and then ran on a treadmill until his legs hurt so badly he couldn't take another step. Every night, he worked himself into a state of fatigue so he could sleep. That was one of the reasons he believed Isaac Phillips when he said he was at the gym every night: Hadrian recognized him.

Once he'd showered and changed into jeans and a T-shirt, he slipped on his leather jacket and stepped out into the fresh night air. The scene could have been on a postcard. Trees swayed in a light breeze, and picturesque buildings stood in the background. The lawns were well-manicured, and the streets lit well and clean.

As the youngest officer in the LAPD to ever make

detective, he'd had his future planned. He would rise in the force, making sergeant, director, special assistant, chief of staff, and eventually, he hoped, chief. After that, former chiefs usually sat on the Board of Commissioners, but there was no real police work there. The board debated issues for the sake of debating.

But the chief... the chief could make a real difference.

A single dash of madness had ended that entire life, and now he was with an agency no one knew anything about, that did the work no one else wanted to do.

He thought about the agency that found him after: Building 4. The one not listed on any directories, with no failures or accomplishments to their name. The one that drifted like a ghost through the halls of government, making its presence known only by the effects of its actions.

He didn't feel like going home, so he went to the Grill. Spirit Lake didn't offer many comfortable places to hang out, but the Grill always had a welcoming atmosphere, even when it was filled to the brim.

Hadrian saw two men outside, one with his arm around the other as they walked away into the dark. One of the men wore black from head to toe, and he was whispering in the other's ear. Hadrian thought it odd, but everything about this little town was odd. He ignored it and continued toward the door.

He went into the Grill and found a table by the window. He sat down and placed the file he'd had under his arm on the tabletop. He ordered a coffee with milk.

The file was on Rebecca Nelson. He opened it and

read about her life. Nothing in there indicated she'd ever crossed paths with anyone that could do this. No drug charges, no juvenile criminal history at all. She volunteered at her church and had a part-time job as a cashier at the local car wash. Her parents were divorced, and she lived with her mother in Spirit Lake. Her father had moved to Richmond.

He closed the file and sat back in the seat, staring out the window as a car passed, its headlights appearing and disappearing as it executed a U-turn.

"Hi."

He turned to see Sayer standing there with a wide smile. "Hey."

"Um… so, this seat taken?"

"No," he said.

She sat across from him. "Did you get the stain out of your jeans?"

"I did, yeah. Thanks."

An awkward silence. Hadrian thought of what Isaac had said about no law against dating a minor, and he felt guilty for thinking it.

"Have you lived in Spirit Lake your whole life?" he asked.

"Yup. Born and bred. My Grams lives here now, so I spend a lot of time with her."

He nodded. "I never knew my grandparents."

"Really? How come?"

"I was an orphan."

"Oh, I'm so sorry."

"No, don't be. It sounds worse than it was. I had a great foster family, and when I hit eighteen, I was admitted to the LAPD, and they became my new family."

She smiled, and it made his heart drop. "Really? A cop at eighteen? That's so young."

"They usually require you to be twenty-one, but they made an exception for me."

"Why?"

Hadrian got a sugar packet out and twirled it in his fingers. "I helped on something. Something that helped out the chief of police. He got an exception for me."

"What'd you help on?"

"I caught someone that had kidnapped and... hurt his daughter."

"Whoa."

"Well, don't let it impress you too much because I've had plenty of screw-ups since."

She grinned. "So, you knew you wanted to be a cop your whole life?"

"Pretty much."

"I wish I had that. That certainty. I have no idea what I want to do. Who knows? I may not even leave Spirit Lake."

"I doubt that. A pretty girl like you..."

They both smiled.

"Sorry," Hadrian said.

"No, it's adorable when you blush."

He cleared his throat. "Listen, Sayer, you're a nice girl, but I can't... I mean, I don't think this should go further than talking. I just want to make sure you understand that."

"Oh, you're with someone, sorry. That was stupid of me. I'm always—"

"It's not that. It's your age."

"I'm eighteen, thank you very much."

"Really?"

"February fifteenth. And I'm not that much younger than you, by the way. How old are you anyway?"

He blushed again. "Twenty-three."

"Five years?" she said, raising an eyebrow. "You're upset about five years?"

"Sorry. That was... I haven't done this in a long time."

"Done what?"

"Liked somebody." A pause. "Look who's blushing now?"

She laughed. "Oh, man."

"Well, if you wanna spend time with an old man, Sayer Bellamy, I would love to take you to dinner and a movie on Saturday."

"I would like that."

Jordan walked over to the table. "Sadie, hey."

"Oh, hey, what're you doing here?"

"I'm here with Remy. Who's your friend?"

"Oh, Hadrian Brams, this is Jordan Lynn. My best friend."

"Hi, Jordan."

"I've seen you around actually. You work with the sheriff."

"I do indeed."

"Well, I didn't want to interrupt. I just wanted to say hi. We're going to my house to watch movies if you guys want to come."

Sayer glanced at Hadrian.

"Sorry," he said. "I have some work I need to do."

"At ten at night?"

"Yeah, justice never sleeps and all. But you go," he said to Sayer. "I should head out now anyway."

"You sure?"

"Yeah. I'll pick you up Saturday. Oh, I guess we should exchange numbers."

She took his hand and the pen that was on top of Rebecca's file and wrote her number on his palm. "Bye," she said with a grin.

Hadrian watched as Jordan and Sayer exchanged glances, and he heard Jordan say, "He's cute."

He blushed again and glanced down to the table. A crime scene photo was sticking out of the file, the pale hand of Rebecca's corpse reaching for something she never got. He closed it and looked back at Sayer. He wondered if she would be just as interested in him if she knew who he really worked for and why he was really here.

10

Remy opened his web browser, and the first thing he saw was a news story about another woman found dead. She had been torn apart, the article said, with so many wounds the coroner had had a difficult time counting them all. He saw a photo of her: young and pretty, just like Jerreck liked.

He rose and went outside. Jerreck was sitting on the porch, texting somebody.

"Who are you texting? You don't have any friends."

"Wow. Someone woke up on the wrong side of the coffin."

Remy looked out past the trees to the road. He remembered this house from decades ago. One of the most challenging things about aging was watching change. In the last century, the world changed more than it had in the past five thousand. Occasionally, the change would get to him, and he would feel disoriented. Out of place somehow. He imagined that's what time travelers would feel like. A tightness would take over his chest, and he'd have to sit somewhere quiet and calm himself.

"Hello, Remy, you still with us?"

"They found another girl."

"Stabbed to death?"

"Yeah."

"That *is* a coincidence."

"It sure is," he said, stepping off the porch and facing Jerreck so he could see his eyes. "You wouldn't happen to know anything about this coincidence, would you?"

"I already told you I didn't do it."

"It just seems a little odd. You're not here a week and we've had four murders."

"Two were mine. Two were not. If you think I have any reason to hide that from you, you're mistaken. It's that pesky morality of yours. Your stubborn refusal to drink human blood. See, I'm just so much stronger than you that I don't have to be scared of anything you can do."

Remy put his hands in his pockets. "They're going to know, Jerreck. This isn't Baltimore or LA, somewhere where murders happen all the time. You keep doing this and the Building 4 Ghosts will know, and *they* will hunt us down and kill us. This town has a history of vampires. The Ghosts somehow are just… sensitive to us. They know our movements. They're keeping track of us." He swallowed. "You keep killing, and they will come for us."

"Ah yes, the perennial boogeymen of Building 4. I hate that name for them, Ghosts. Couldn't they choose something more original? Or just go with 'agents' and be as boring as everybody else?"

"It's not a joke."

"Everything's a joke, little brother. Especially secret government agencies hiding in the shadows taking notes on what vampires are doing." He leaned forward. "You know what, Rems, I've lived more than a century and a half, killed hundreds of people, and I have never once seen anyone from this mysterious Building 4 of yours that makes you cower under the sheets at night."

"I've seen them. They're real, and they know about us. I don't know why they don't just wipe us all out, they know how, but they have something planned. And whatever it is, it won't be good for us."

He inhaled deeply, unimpressed, and said, "Well, if it helps, I swear, on that little morsel Jordan that you seem to have fallen for already, that I did not kill those girls."

Remy considered him for a moment. "I believe you."

"Thank you."

Remy exhaled and sat down next to him. "I'm going to help them."

"Who?"

"The police. I'm going to help them find whoever's killing these girls."

"Vampire detective? Cool comic book maybe, but *no bueno* in real life."

"I'm serious, Jerreck. Someone might think this was vampires. And it's the right thing to do."

He rolled his eyes. "You're not going to start into another lecture about ethics, are you? Cause I'll let you in on a secret, little brother, there is no morality. I've traveled the world, sat at the feet of masters, talked with vampires a millennia-old, and I did not see morality. In people, or in us. We're beyond it. And the sooner you realize that, the better. Because not having it is a huge evolutionary advantage."

"Sure. Just ask all the extinct species that were too selfish to worry about their kind. Now you going to help me or not?"

"Help the police find a killer? I am a killer, Remy. Much worse than the one they're looking for." He rose. "Now if you'll excuse me, I have to get ready for a date. She's going to be quite tasty."

"Jerreck—"

"I'm not going to kill her. I'll just suck a little and compel her to forget. Easy peasy. You really should look into it."

Remy watched him go. A deep, burning desire screamed at him to throw Jerreck out of town. But Jerreck was right. Surviving only on the blood of animals meant he was much weaker than his older brother. If it ever came to a confrontation, Jerreck would come out on top. And right now, he needed his brother's help. If Building 4 was in town, things had just taken a turn for the worst.

He'd dealt with them once in Germany. All he remembered was men in suits with guns that looked like plastic toys, but when they opened fire, the rays of the sun itself seemed to shoot out of them. Even the medallions they all had didn't protect them. Building 4, whoever they were, knew of Remy's kind, knew how to kill them, and yet for a reason he couldn't figure out, let them live.

His cell phone rang. It was Jordan. His heart skipped a beat, and he felt embarrassed to have such a reaction at his age.

"Hey," he said.

"I have to cancel tonight."

"Why?"

"It's my brother. He's high right now."

"Oh."

"He's been doing that a lot since my parents passed away. I've got to stay with him tonight. See if some sisterly time can convince him to cut it out."

"Well, it's for a good cause, at least."

"You're disappointed."

He shook his head even though she couldn't see him. "No, it's fine. Really. Take care of your brother. I had something to do tonight anyway. I'll give you a call tomorrow."

"You sure?"

"Positive."

"Okay. I'll talk to you tomorrow."

He hung up and rose. Bypassing his car, he sprinted so quickly through the trees that a human's eyes wouldn't have been able to pick him up. He ducked under branches and leapt dozens of feet in the air over cars and mailboxes.

Within a few minutes, he was standing in front of the Spirit Lake police station.

11

The file sat open on Hadrian's desk, photos of Amanda and Rebecca side-by-side. He looked at them for a long time, his eyes straining. Sometimes he thought if he could keep his eyes on photos long enough, they would reveal something. But they never did.

"Excuse me, Deputy," the receptionist said.

"Yeah?"

"There's someone here to see you. He says it's about the girls that were killed."

Hadrian rose and went to the front of the station. A young man stood there staring out the windows.

"Can I help you?"

"Yeah, they tell me you're in charge of the investigation into the deaths of Rebecca Nelson and Amanda Sorin."

"Who told you that?"

The young man smiled and took a few steps forward, holding out his hand. "Remy Simone."

Hadrian shook his hand. "Hadrian Brams."

"I'm here to help you, Deputy Brams. I want to make sure the person that killed Amanda and Rebecca is brought to justice."

"How old are you—eighteen?"

"Something like that."

"I think you should go back to school and let the police handle this. Unless, of course, you know something that can help."

"I don't have any information that you don't have. But I have certain skills that would be helpful to you."

"We don't need your help, but I appreciate it. Have a good one." Hadrian turned to leave.

"I googled you."

Hadrian froze.

"Youngest cadet ever let into the academy, youngest officer ever to make detective. Pretty impressive. There was some other stuff, too."

Hadrian turned around. "Remy, I think you should go home and let us handle this."

"You quit without explanation and left the state. What happened?"

"That's none of your business. And I'd like you to leave now."

"Let me help you. I have a specific skill set that you need."

"The ability to annoy me isn't a skill set I need."

"You have a scar on your pinky finger. It's two years old and was caused by some sort of wood."

Hadrian glanced down to the nick between his pinky and ring finger. "How did you see that?"

"Am I right about the wood?"

"It was a splinter from a tree. How did you know that?"

Remy grinned. "I see things other people can't see. That's what you need because we both know this type of killer is going to kill again."

"How do you know that?"

"I have some experience with these types of people."

Hadrian looked Remy up and down. He thought the young man appeared harmless enough, though maybe a little morbid if he was getting involved with this when he didn't have to. "I appreciate the offer. Now please go."

Remy shrugged. "I'll look into it on my own if I have to, but I think the two of us have a better chance of finding him together... Especially if Building 4 is worried about finding him and sent you."

Hadrian watched him leave. He would have to look a little more fully into the background of Remy Simone.

Hadrian spent most of the day dealing with two domestic disturbance calls—both roommates that had gotten into a fight—and then filled out paperwork on some closed cases. He had a trial coming up where he would have to testify, but he guessed he wouldn't be in town long enough to get there.

After the paperwork was done, he put his feet up on the desk for a moment and relaxed. Police work no longer satisfied him. He came to it out of comfort because he wasn't good at anything else, but he knew it wasn't for him early on. When he was recruited by Building 4 and shown things other people only believed existed in fairy tales, that fire he first had was reignited in him. The grunt work he had to do now to fit in was the payment for the real work he did when no one was around.

Vampires were what he was here to look into, and he had a good hunch one just walked in and shook his hand like it was the most normal thing in the world.

He grabbed his gym bag and headed to the gym. After pounding out an hour on the elliptical, he spent a long time in the locker room lying on a bench with his arm over his eyes, blocking the harsh lights.

When he did regain enough strength to move, he leaned on the tiled wall in the shower and let the hot water run over him.

Screams. That's what he heard in his head. The final screams of Amanda Sorin and Rebecca Nelson. He couldn't imagine the horror they had felt as the knife plunged into their bodies. They knew they were going to die and were powerless to stop it. He wondered if they begged for their lives and whether it made the monster smile.

After his shower, he headed to the Grill. He would pass a grocery store on the way home and could have easily picked up some groceries, but the thought of that filled him with a gray dread.

"You've made a friend."

Hadrian stopped and watched the man in the gray suit. He leaned against the wall of the building nearest him, an office building near the Grill, but Hadrian would have sworn he wasn't there before.

"Remy?"

"Yes, Remy. You know what he is, don't you?"

"I do. But I'm not here for him."

"No, but that might change. The one we sent you here for is five hundred years old and may have already fled. Their instincts get sharper the older they get. Keep your eyes open, Agent Brahms. There's more at play here than you think."

Hadrian only looked away for a moment, but the man was gone. Like he had never been there in the first place. He took a deep breath and kept walking.

As he walked in, he scanned the restaurant for Sayer, but she wasn't there. Disappointed more than he thought he would be, he sat at a booth and ordered a turkey sandwich and a Sprite. The food came quickly, and he ate a few bites before he was interrupted.

"It's gotta be someone from the school," Remy said as he sat down across from him.

"What are you doing here?"

"I'm helping. That's what Amanda and Rebecca have in common. They both go to the same school."

"Congratulations, you've cracked the case. Will you go home now?"

"You need my help."

"Why do you think that?"

Remy took a fry off his plate and ate it. "Because no one else around here has dealt with this."

"And you're the expert?"

Remy shrugged. "Maybe I've just been around long

enough to have seen some things."

Hadrian wiped his lips with a napkin. "You seem like a nice guy, Remy. But when civilians help with police investigations, things get complicated. If we catch this guy, you're going to have to testify in court. It's not going to look good to a jury that a high school kid had to help out on our investigation. You could also contaminate evidence. It's not worth the risk." He rose. "Good night."

Hadrian walked outside to his car. Remy was standing next to it.

"How'd you do that?"

"What if I brought you some evidence you've missed?" Remy said. "Then would you consider that I have something to contribute?"

"And how would you know about evidence that I've missed?"

"Leave that to me. But if I find something, will you consider letting me help you?"

He thought about that for a moment. "Sure. I'll consider it."

Remy grinned. "See you in a bit then."

12

When night fell over Spirit Lake, it was as sudden as a light switching off. Some of the residents said it fell much more quickly there than anywhere else they'd been, and there were infinite theories as to why. The longitudinal location of the city, the elevation, etc. But no one ever came up with a valid reason that satisfied everyone.

But as Lucian stood outside the party, he was glad night did fall so quickly.

He felt more comfortable at night. Like he could hide in plain sight.

The party was packed, and it seemed like everyone in town who was under the age of twenty-five was there. The house, belonging to someone Lucian had never spoken to, was filled with people, and they spilled out onto the front lawn, cups of beer in hand.

Glancing back to Jerreck, seeing that mischievous smile, he wondered what the hell he was doing there.

"I don't like parties," Lucian said.

"You need to socialize more," Jerreck said.

"Why?"

"Because you're the weird quiet kid right now. If they come asking questions at the school, the weird quiet kid is who they're coming to first." He slapped his back. "Come on, you might have fun."

The party was loud, and the house smelled like beer and vomit. Several people were making out on couches, but most everyone else was wandering around or dancing or trying to hear what the person next to them was saying. In the kitchen, he saw a few people he knew—Vicky and Rich and a kid named Ian— smoking pot.

"I really don't like it here," he said. "I'd rather be in a library."

"Weird quiet kid, remember? Now, let's see how you do with the ladies. About half of them looked over to us when we walked in. I assume it was mostly because of me, but I'm sure some of them were looking at you."

"What do you want me to do?"

"Talk to them. I want to see what I have to work with. That blonde one right there keeps looking back at you."

Lucian saw the girl. She was stunningly beautiful but with a little too much makeup. He walked over after a nudge from Jerreck.

"Um… cool party, right?" he said.

"Yeah."

Lucian thought back to the television shows he ab- sorbed on a daily basis. What would the Fonz say to this girl?

"So what say you we get outta here?"

"I'm with my friends."

"Oh," he said. "No, I didn't mean, I mean, I meant it but I didn't mean—"

Jerreck put his arm around him and pulled him away.

"That was even painful for me to watch."

"I told you I've never been good with girls."

Jerreck turned him around, so they were looking eye-to-eye. "I saw what you did to Amanda. That was pure power, pure animalistic rage. That's what you need to tap. When you're speaking to a girl, don't see her as a girl. She's an object there for you to seduce and to use however you see fit. She's there for you and only you. Got it?"

He nodded.

"Good. Now go get 'em."

Lucian felt dizzy and stood awkwardly for a few moments. Then he went across the room to a brunette who was sitting on the stairs leading up to the second floor.

He stood before her until she noticed him. He closed his eyes for a second, and when he opened them, a smile came over his lips. "Tammy, right?" he said.

"Yeah."

"I don't think we've officially met, I'm Lucian."

"Oh, right. You're in French with me."

"That's right, I am."

He smiled widely, and it made her blush.

Lucian tasted her lip gloss as he kissed her. They were outside, leaning against Tammy's car. She was soft under his roaming hands, and she didn't stop him. She didn't yell or scream or try to hit him. She was enjoying it.

He bit down on her lip, and she groaned. He did it again, but this time when he pulled away, he tasted blood.

She yelped.

He didn't stop. He pinned her against the car, his hand to her throat, and squeezed until she started to struggle. Suddenly, he felt a force against his shoulder, and then he was thrown back on the cement.

"What the hell do you think you're doing?" Jerreck said.

Lucian was on his feet, Tammy's blood dripping from his mouth. "You wanted me to kill her."

"I didn't want you to kill her."

Tammy was hysterical. Jerreck brought her close and looked into her eyes. She went quiet.

"You won't remember this," he said. "You got too drunk at the party and passed out on the lawn."

"I got drunk and passed out on the lawn," she said.

"Good. Now go away."

Lucian looked from her to Jerreck. "What was that?"

"Forget that. You were going to kill her."

"Isn't that what we're doing?"

"No. Fifty people saw you leave the party with her.

This was an exercise to make you comfortable around women. To learn to seduce them. What were you thinking?"

He wiped the blood away with the back of his hand. "It was nice. She liked me kissing her. I just got excited."

Jerreck exhaled. "I think we have a long way to go still before you're ready."

"Ready for what?"

"Ready to be like me."

13

Morgues had always made Remy Simone uncomfortable. Being a vampire who was uncomfortable around death was weird, but it was true. Sometimes he felt almost human, and maybe places like morgues reminded him that he was something else.

He walked to the front counter and took off his sunglasses. An overweight man in glasses with food stains on his shirt was reading a hardcover book and took no notice of him.

"Excuse me," Remy said. "I'm here to see the body of Amanda Sorin."

Looking up from his book, he said, "You a cop?"

"Nope. Well, I was once. But not now."

"You a doctor?"

"Nope."

"Family?"

"No, just here to see the body."

"Can't do that."

Remy leaned in, and their eyes locked. "You're going

to take me back to the body and give me time with it."

"I'll take you back," the man said with a sigh as he placed his book down. "Come on."

Remy followed him through some double doors and down a long corridor with offices on either side. People had motivational posters up on their walls. A common area with a coffee maker and microwave sat empty but messy.

They took the elevator down, and the doors opened onto a floor that looked like a hospital basement. They entered a room with metal gurneys. Blue tarps covered the bodies—Remy could smell the decay—and Amanda's was there.

"They're having the funeral tomorrow, so you came at the right time."

"Thanks," Remy said. "Give me some time alone if you don't mind."

"Sure."

Remy waited until the man left before approaching the body. He'd been there before, or someplace exactly the same anyway, many times. When he lived in London in the early twentieth century, he had worked briefly with Scotland Yard. The Sherlock Holmes books had inspired him, and he'd thought he'd give it a shot. But he hadn't been prepared for what he saw.

The sheer cruelty that people showed each other was astounding. Parents murdering children, lovers killing each other… cruelty for pleasure. It was everything he fought against. Fought against now, anyway. Then, he enjoyed it. He relished it… and took part in it. Being a member of Scotland Yard, he was above suspicion and killed and ate more people than he could count.

But there were a few cases then that piqued his interest, and he actually worked them. And as he had been working those cases, trying to find the links between victims and see them how their killers saw them, he thought of his brother Jerreck.

Jerreck was hot-tempered and without remorse. He killed even when he wasn't hungry. He enjoyed it, maybe even more than the blood. The thought that his own brother could do that filled Remy with revulsion, and he had to force himself to stop thinking about him.

They had to escape from London in 1911. Jerreck had said people were simply on high alert, and the chances of detection were now too high, but Remy knew it was something else. Something subterranean. It was the first inkling he had received about Building 4. About a society that knew things about the world the rest of humanity did not.

He removed the blue tarp. The flesh was stiff and gray, and her eyes were closed. The wounds were a dark purple, and they covered her nude body from the hips up to the neck. Taking a step back and folding his arms, he stared at her with his vampire eyes.

Being human wasn't something he remembered well, other than in his dreams. Remy didn't know what this body would appear like to someone with ordinary eyes, but to him, it was beautiful. Everything was. Occasionally, he found himself staring intently at a ladybug or a cloud. The colors on a penny were as vibrant as the sun, and he could see the ridges, the indentations, the scuff marks... nothing was hidden from him. Watching the world, he would lose track of time and notice later that he'd lost three hours gazing at a leaf with dew dripping from it.

The wounds were small slits. Examining each one, his eyes drifted, seeing inside them, past the flesh and down to the bone. As he came up to the hips, he stopped. Something was there. He looked around for tools and saw some on a counter. Going through them, he moved aside the drills and cutting instruments, the scales and syringes, and found several tweezers in a plastic case. He picked the smallest one and pulled a small baggie from a carton next to the tools.

Reaching the tweezers into the wound, he kept his eyes on the shimmering sliver he had seen. He pulled it out, placed it in the baggie, and then held it up to the light. A fragment of metal from the knife that killed her.

He placed the baggie in his pocket and turned his attention back to the body. He pulled the tarp up to her neck and gazed down at her passive face.

I'm sorry.

Remy turned and walked out of the morgue.

14

Hadrian left his apartment and was locking the door when the hairs on the nape of his neck stood up. Turning, he saw Remy standing behind him with a grin on his face. A little baggie was in his hand, and he held it up.

"What's that?" Hadrian asked.

"The evidence, as promised."

"What is it?"

"A piece of the murder weapon. Should tell the county labs what type of knife, and then we can track down where it was bought." He handed the bag over, and Hadrian took it. "Do I get to help out now?"

"How do I know you didn't just lift some piece of metal off the street?"

"I promise you, that is from the murder weapon."

"How did you get it?"

"Oh, I see. You think I killed them and I'm toying with you now. Rebecca was killed, according to your own coroner, almost a month ago now. I've been in town exactly three weeks. Check with the school. Check with my uncle Rich."

"Don't think I won't."

"Please do."

Hadrian looked at the plastic baggie and said, "Thanks," before walking out to his car and getting in. The passenger door opened, and Remy got in, too.

"Remy—"

"Both girls went to the same school. We need to find —"

"A class they were both in, I know."

"See, great minds think alike."

"You're not coming with me," he said, placing the key in the ignition but not turning the car on.

"I go to that school. I can help you, trust me."

"I don't even know you, how am I supposed to trust you?"

"You're thinking of a Venn diagram, aren't you?"

Hadrian was silent.

Remy leaned in a little, his face bright. "Look at all the victims and see where in their lives they overlap, and that's where the killer is. I've done that before, too. I can help you find that overlap."

"What's in this for you? Why do you care?"

Remy looked out the windshield at some kids crossing the street. "I need a reason to help get a killer off the streets?"

"Most kids your age don't give a damn about anything that's happening to someone else. They're too self-absorbed to worry about it."

"Let's just say I'm mature for my age. So we going to

the school or what?"

Hadrian hesitated and then started the car.

The interior of Spirit Lake High School was like any other high school Hadrian had ever seen. But he'd only ever been to them during investigations. He'd tested out when he was twelve and began taking college credit. But now, seeing the girls and hearing the party planning for next weekend and the complaints about homework and teachers and the discussion about the football season, he truly felt he had missed out.

"Where did you go to high school?" Remy said.

"Didn't it say in your google results?"

"No, actually."

Walking down the hall, they had to make way for two boys chasing each other, one of them with a section of hair shaved that he no doubt hadn't consented to.

"I tested out."

"Really? You must be smart. Building 4 only recruits geniuses, I hear. Not just smart, but like actual geniuses."

Hadrian grabbed him and shoved something the size of a pin into his arm. Remy's head flew back, and his body froze, the veins underneath his skin seemed to be forcing their way out and, throbbing, looked like they were about to burst. Blood began to trickle out of his eyes and ears.

"You ever say that name again, and I will end you. Are we clear?"

He couldn't respond. Hadrian withdrew the needle.

Remy collapsed onto the ground. His color, pale as it was, returned to him, and his veins vanished. He got to his feet eventually and leaned against the wall. "What was that?" he said, barely able to speak. "I've never felt anything like it."

"Mention my employer again, vampire, and you'll have a lot more of it."

They continued down the hall in silence. A guy and girl were making out against the lockers and gave them a dirty look.

The administration offices were around the corner, and they went inside and waited until the receptionist had finished a phone call. She looked up and said, "May I help you?"

"Yeah, I'm Deputy Brahms with the Sheriff's Office. I need the school schedules for Amanda Sorin and Rebecca Nelson, please."

"Oh, sorry, but I can't give those out."

"But they're dead."

"I know that, but we have a strict policy here."

"What if I get the parents' permission?"

"You can have the parents pick it up and give it to you if you want, but I can't release it to anyone else."

"That's going to take too much time. Is there anything else I can do? What if I saw the judge for an order?"

Remy said, "That won't be necessary. Right? You will give us the schedules that we ask for."

The receptionist was silent for a long time, staring unblinkingly at Remy. "Of course. Let me print them off."

Hadrian glanced at Remy, but he just smiled and sat down on a chair against the wall.

Once the documents had been brought out, Hadrian sat next to him and compared the two schedules. Only one class was the same: third period American history.

"That's it," Remy said.

"That's what?"

"Where the killer is. Third period history."

Hadrian exhaled and folded the schedules up, staring at Remy. "You're not going in there with me."

"I wouldn't think of it. Besides, third period's out. You'll have to wait until tomorrow. But you should grab a list of the students in the class now. I have a feeling the receptionist may not be in such a good mood later."

15

Twilight. Nine o'clock and only now was the sun starting to set. Some summer days in Spirit Lake were incredibly long.

Lucian walked through a neighborhood by the school, a girl by the name of Stephanie walking alongside him. His conversation with her was smooth, and several times he made her laugh. Jerreck had told him to watch for the touch, that girls would never touch a guy they weren't attracted to. It took forty minutes of walking and a milkshake, but finally, she touched his arm after he said something funny.

"You wanna come back to my house?" Lucian asked. "We can just hang and watch a movie."

"I would, but I have so much homework."

"It'll still be there later tonight. Come on, this kind of moment is what life's made of. Let's seize it. Come back with me. I'll introduce you to my grandma, you'll like her."

She nibbled on her lip. "Okay, why not. One movie."

"One movie." He looked down an alleyway. "I know a shortcut. Let's go this way."

This was the moment that made his stomach churn and his heart pound in his ears. The moment when he asked them to come with him willingly. It had worked twice before and had failed dozens of times. But he reached his hand out to be taken by the soft hand of the girl walking next to him… and it worked.

The alley was dark, a brick wall to one side, and to the other man-sized bushes and hedges bordering a line of homes. But Lucian had walked this route a hundred times and never seen anyone in any of the houses. They were likely abandoned.

"Wait," he said when they had gone far enough in that no one would be able to hear them. "I have something to give you."

"What is it?"

Without a moment's hesitation, he shoved her down and climbed on top of her. He pulled out his knife and went to thrust it down, but her hands were wrapped around his wrist, stopping him. Then she screamed and clawed his eyes. The pain was blinding, and he yelped as she rolled away and took off down the alley.

He tried to follow, but the pain in his eyes hobbled him. He had to crouch down and just take it.

In the shadows, Jerreck had the girl by the throat. He dragged her back and threw her next to Lucian.

"That was sloppy."

"She scratched my eyes."

Jerreck shook his head. "The kill should be clean

and efficient. They should never see it coming."

"How would you know?"

Jerreck smirked. Too quickly for Lucian to see, he lifted the girl. Fangs appeared in his mouth, his eyes burned red, veins protruded from his face.

Jerreck tore into the girl's throat, blood spattering over cement and Lucian's clothing. The girl moaned in ecstasy for a long while, and then she went silent. Jerreck let her flop on the ground.

"That's how you kill somebody," he said. Then he stumbled to the ground and leaned back on his hands. He appeared dazed.

Lucian slowly moved away from him. "What the hell are you?"

"Really? I just drank her blood and you have no clue?"

"But that can't be true," Lucian said, his voice trembling.

"Oh, it's true. And it is really, really good."

"What do you want with me?"

He grinned, his eyebrows fluttering with excitement. "I'm going to turn you."

"Turn me? Into... one of you?"

"Exactamundo."

"Why me?"

"Well, honestly, I'm just bored. And my holier-than-thou brother isn't as fun as he used to be. He was always the life of the party, the one to get the hottest girls and boys and kill them. But now it's 'human life is valuable' this and 'you can't just murder people for fun' that. He's really wrinkling my ass." He wiped the blood from his chin with his hand. "But you... you, Lucian, are going to be a lot of fun. Me and you, we're going to show people why they're afraid of the dark."

16

The night always welcomed him. No matter how horrible the day had been, no matter how much pain it had been filled with, the night was always there. Like a lover that waited for you in the shadows, never judging, never rejecting.

Jerreck Simone loved the night. As he sat on the roof of their home, watching the town that had become a place he loathed rather than longed to get back to, he heard a car from nearly half a mile away.

Jordan pulled up with Remy in the passenger seat. Though they spoke quietly, Jerreck could hear them. They were talking about school, about their dreams, about their desires, and what they meant. They were falling in love.

Next to him, Jerreck had a photo. It belonged to Remy. He kept it hidden away and didn't know that Jerreck knew about it. A simple photo taken in 1864 of a young woman, Bethany Hatton. She was, in every physical aspect, identical to Jordan. Remy would never admit it to himself, but he was falling in love with Bethany again.

But Bethany, at least as far as the world at large knew, had burned in a fire in 1864. Set by founding members of Spirit Lake on a vampire-killing rampage.

She had been the one to turn both Jerreck and Remy. Remy thought he had been the one she wanted, but Jerreck knew that wasn't true. His love for Bethany had been pure, and she loved him back. She told him so. But an uncomfortable feeling gnawed at his gut that maybe she loved Remy, too… and Jerreck hated him for it.

Remy and Jordan kissed, and it sent an icy chill down Jerreck's back, like a cold finger running along his spine. He had to look away, look at the photo of Bethany for as long as he could.

Eventually, he silently hopped off the roof and headed to Antonio's Bar & Grill. There was nowhere else to hang out in this one-horse town.

He entered, and the scent of humans was intoxicating. Nothing smelled the same once you were a vampire. The sensations were so intense that sometimes he couldn't take it. The scents and sights and sounds, amplified to the degree that was unimaginable to a human, melded and distorted in his mind and caused a jumble of sensation. Only through patience and careful concentration was he able to separate it all when the overwhelming feelings came. He wondered how he had gotten through it when he had been a younger vampire.

Then again, there wasn't so much noise nearly two centuries ago. No jets, planes, cars, cell phones, speakers… nothing but human voices and nature.

He sat at the bar and ordered a whiskey. Alcohol helped warm the body of a vampire, which was naturally cold. Caffeine could help, too. Jerreck sipped the whiskey and savored its taste on his tongue before asking for less ice.

Though he'd fed today, the hunger pangs were coming back. Some days, he was nothing but hunger. It took over every emotion, every sense, and every thought. He'd never admit this to Remy, but he was impressed that Remy could control it. And even jealous. He had never been able to control it. He was always its slave.

A young brunette next to him ordered two drinks, and Jerreck turned to her. "Hi," he said, with his broadest smile.

She smiled back but didn't say anything.

"I'm Jerreck."

"Natalie."

"So, Natalie, I'm new in town. Do you guys have anywhere else, anywhere at all, that you congregate other than this restaurant?"

"No offense, but I'm here with my boyfriend, so you don't need to try."

"I can't be nice without wanting to get into your pants?"

She turned away from him.

"Natalie, look at me. I have something for you." She turned to him, her pupils dilating as she locked eyes with him. "You're going to tell your boyfriend you don't really like him anymore. He's going to resist, and you're going to tell him that you'll talk to him about it tomorrow, but that you're going home with me tonight. Then you're going to come over and sit down."

He glanced away and took a sip of his drink.

"Excuse me," she said, "I have to break up with my boyfriend. Do you mind if I go home with you tonight?"

"Funny you should ask. I was just going to suggest the same thing."

"Great. I'll be right back."

Jerreck watched as she gave her boyfriend the bad news. His face was priceless, and Jerreck laughed out loud. As Natalie walked back to him, the boyfriend grabbed her arm, trying to force a conversation.

"Excuse me, bartender?" Jerreck said to a young man. "I think that gentleman there is harassing that girl."

The bartender went over and confronted the boyfriend, who was losing it at this point. The manager had to get involved, too, and they took the boyfriend by his arms and dragged him out. Natalie composed herself and came to sit next to him.

"So," she said. "Where were we?"

"I feel like sitting in a hot tub. Do you have one at your house?"

"No, but my friend does. I'm sure she wouldn't mind."

As he soaked in the heated water, Jerreck leaned back and watched the stars. Sometimes he was so obsessed with eating that he would forget how beautiful the world could really be. A door opened from inside the house, and Natalie's friend led Lucian to the tub.

"There he is," Jerreck said. "Take your clothes off and get in."

Lucian didn't move for a moment. He eventually stripped down to his boxer shorts and stepped into the hot tub. "Why did you text me?" he asked.

"I wanted you to join us. Lucian, this is Natalie. Natalie, Lucian. This is the boy we talked about. The one that's going to kill you."

"Oh, cool. It's nice to meet you."

Lucian sat frozen. "What did you do to her?"

"You humans have feeble minds. They're not that difficult to control." He took a kitchen knife off the side of the hot tub and handed it to Lucian. "Now you're going to do it right. No frantic stabbing like she's a piñata. One strike, like a cobra." He reached over and touched just under Natalie's ribcage by her heart. "One strike here and then pull the knife out. She'll both suffocate and bleed to death."

Lucian swallowed hard. He edged over to the girl, who was smiling widely and looking him in the eyes.

"Do it, Lucian."

"I can't. She's smiling at me."

"So what?"

"So there should be screams or something."

"Oh, you like the screams. Okay. Natalie, be a dear and scream your head off."

Natalie screamed so loudly lights went on in the houses surrounding them. Lucian panicked and tried to quiet her. But she kept screaming, loud enough that she started going hoarse.

"Please, be quiet! You have to be quiet!"

"She's not going to be, Lucian, and the neighbors are getting curious. You better put an end to this quickly."

He begged and pleaded, but she wouldn't stop. A neighbor shouted something from a backyard. Lucian plunged the knife into Natalie's heart, and she gasped. As if a spell had been broken, her eyes went wide with terror, and she cried as she saw the blade sticking out of her chest.

"Now, pull it out."

Lucian did as he was told, and Jerreck leaned down and drank from the hole in the heart. No two people's blood ever tasted the same. Their lifestyles, eating habits, diseases, age, stress levels... all of it altered the taste.

Natalie's had a sweet taste, like a dessert wine, and was slightly fragranced. He drank until his belly hurt and then pulled away, Natalie turning white as marble.

"Man, that was good." He breathed deeply and leaned against the hot tub again. "You see, Lucian, how much quicker and easier that was? One precise blow. Nothing else is needed." He looked at him. "You got something to say to me, so just say it. What is it?"

Lucian said, "I want to do it again."

Jerreck couldn't help but smile.

17

Hadrian wore jeans and a leather jacket to the school the next morning rather than his uniform. He didn't want anyone to be aware that he was there on business. The man in the gray suit had messaged him last night. All it said was that he was running out of time, and they needed him elsewhere. Two days and Building 4 would withdraw him.

How many more people will die if I'm reassigned?

Walking the halls again, the sting of the youthful years Hadrian missed out on came back. He'd never been married or in a serious relationship. But now he felt like he could have been if he'd had someplace he could've met women instead of working for a government organization that moved him every three or four weeks.

He had been recognized by Building 4 early, as part of a program they never really explained to him. At the age of sixteen, he was taken from his parents and moved to a training facility in Washington. Where he saw and learned things that he thought only existed in fairy tales. Then he was returned to Los Angeles at eighteen, and secured a job as a police officer at an age it was illegal to be one. It seemed to him at the time that Building 4 could do whatever they wanted, and his opinion hadn't changed much since.

Second period was out, and third was just beginning.

Hadrian waited by the school administration office until the bell sounded. The halls cleared in less than a minute, and he rose and went to the classroom. Kids were getting settled, and the teacher, a woman in a skirt and Crocs, looked up at him from her paperwork. He walked to her and leaned down, showing the badge.

"Can we speak in the hall, please?"

"Certainly."

Hadrian stepped a few paces away from the door and waited for the teacher to do the same.

"I got a copy of the roll last night. Amanda Ronin and Rebecca Nelson were both in this class, right?"

She got a solemn look on her face. "Yes, they were."

"On the roll, there was another girl, a Heidi Plumworth, and there was a note that said she had received a fail due to excessive unexplained absences. Is she here now?"

"No, she hasn't been to class for almost three weeks."

"Have you had contact with her or her family?"

"She lives with her father, but he hasn't seen her. Didn't seem too concerned about it when I spoke to him." She looked around before whispering, "He's a Jehovah's Witness."

He nodded, though he had no idea what that was supposed to mean. "I need to speak to some of your students."

"May I ask why?"

"Because one of them killed those two girls, and probably Heidi, too."

She looked shocked and didn't say anything, so Hadrian slid past her into the classroom. He stood at the doorway and examined the boys. Eleven of them. A few glanced up but were mostly uninterested. A couple were flirting with the girls next to them; some were doodling.

One boy in the back had his head down, his foot tapping manically against the floor. He looked up and then quickly down again. Hadrian walked over to him.

"What's your name?"

"Um, Lucian."

"Right, Lucian Cody. Hey, do you mind stepping out with me really quick? We need to chat."

"What about?"

Hadrian moved his jacket aside, revealing the badge clipped to his waistband. "It's about some girls that were in this class."

Lucian hesitated then nodded. "Sure."

As Lucian rose, a fist flew at Hadrian out of nowhere and bashed into his jaw. He hit the floor hard and watched Lucian sprint out of the classroom. His vision was blurry, but he got to his feet among the shocked murmurs of the other students. He ran out of the classroom.

The squeaking footfalls ahead of him led to the front entrance. Hadrian ran toward them. He pushed through the doors and saw Lucian running around the school onto a public road. Hadrian followed.

A car horn blared, and brakes squealed as someone barely avoided running Lucian over. Hadrian pumped his arms, and his legs burned as he dashed across the street into a nearby park.

Lucian was sprinting across the grass. He looked back and nearly fell over. Hadrian was faster than he was.

Lucian jumped onto a fence and climbed over. Hadrian got there only a moment later and hopped over it, seemingly landing in a sprint. He turned the corner, and a rock flew at him. It nailed him in the cheek, and he stumbled back, holding his face.

Lucian turned and ran, and Hadrian was after him again, ignoring the pain. He was close now, no more than a few feet. He could hear Lucian huffing and puffing, clearly exhausted.

Hadrian tackled him on the sidewalk. Both men rolled several times. Hadrian finally held Lucian down by his neck as he struggled and grunted. He got both arms loose and struck Hadrian several times in the face. He rolled Hadrian onto his back.

Lucian rose and kicked him in the ribs and the head before taking off again. Hadrian was seeing stars and felt pain across his chest. He turned onto his stomach and looked up at the escaping boy. Then he saw Lucian come to an abrupt stop.

Remy Simone stood there with his hand on Lucian's

throat. Remy pushed him down to the ground effort-
lessly and held him there.

18

Hadrian stepped out of his office and saw Remy sitting in the lounge, flipping through a magazine. He came and sat next to him, an ice pack on his face.

"You okay?" Remy asked.

"I'll live. He's strong for a skinny guy."

"Yeah, well, don't underestimate us skinny guys."

"Thanks, Remy. For all your help."

"You're welcome."

Hadrian rose. "He's been read his rights, and I'm about to interview him. You can come back with me but just as an observer. No questions. If you have any questions, tell them to me and I'll ask him. Got it?"

"Got it."

"Okay, come on."

He led Remy back to the interview room and opened the door. Lucian sat there, nervously tapping the desk. Remy went to a chair in the corner, and Hadrian sat across from Lucian, setting down a manila envelope.

"Lucian, I know you're scared, but you don't need to be. I'm not here to hurt you or do anything to harm you. Do you understand that?"

Lucian nodded.

"Good. I want to talk to you about Amanda Sorin. We already know you did it, Lucian. We know you killed her. We can move past that." He pulled out a plastic baggie from the manila envelope. Inside was a couple of strands of hair, the same color as Lucian's. "This is your hair. We found it on the body of Amanda Sorin. I'm getting a warrant to take a hair sample from you and prove that it's yours. After that, I'll have all the evidence I need. No more deals after that. Do you understand?"

Lucian nodded.

"I want to help you, Lucian. I'm going to help you. Like I said, we already know you did it. What I don't get is why? But I think I can guess. No one can piss you off like girls. I had this girlfriend once that as soon as she came home, she demanded that whatever I was watching had to be turned off so she could put on country music. And I didn't want to listen to country music at six o'clock at night. I wanted to watch baseball. And she'd smoke when I asked her not to, she'd take my car out and bring it back without any gas... I thought about killing her. I just never had the guts, you know? I thought it'd be too hard." He leaned forward. "Is it, Lucian? Is it hard to do?"

Lucian glanced at Remy and then back. "No, it's not hard. I thought it would be, too."

"Was Amanda the first?"

"Yes."

"And Heidi was the latest?"

"Yes."

"She's pretty. I bet it was exciting. How'd you do it?"

Lucian grinned slightly. It made Hadrian's stomach churn.

"I told her I needed a tutor, a math tutor. She never bothered to check that I was in AP calculus. She came over to my house, and I took her out to the backyard. This was when my Ma wasn't home. Heidi was bent down over this math book, and I stuck the knife into her. It was in her neck. She jumped up and touched the hole in her neck and just gave me this look. It was like… just shock. I'd never seen anyone give me that kind of look."

"What'd you do then?"

"I kept stabbing. I got her face a lot. I didn't want to, but I couldn't stop. She started running around the yard, and I just kept stabbing her. Then she fell down and didn't get up again."

Hadrian nodded and pulled a legal pad and pen close, glancing up to the camera in the corner. "Lucian, I'd like to start from the beginning and have you take me through what happened to all three girls."

Afternoon came and went before Hadrian was done. He ordered Chinese takeout, and he, Lucian, and Remy ate and talked. They took a break at about three o'clock and shared some sodas and then wrapped up around four.

"So, what's going to happen now?" Lucian asked.

"That's going to be up to the DA. But I'm putting in a good word for you, Lucian. I'm going to let him know that you were fully cooperative."

"Okay. So can I go home now?"

Hadrian was silent for a moment. "Afraid not, buddy. Just hang tight for a minute."

Hadrian and Remy walked out of the room, and Remy turned to him and said, "I feel bad for him."

"Why?"

"I don't think he understands what's going on."

"He murdered three girls and doesn't feel an ounce of remorse. I'll be able to sleep just fine."

Remy nodded, glancing down. "I better take off. I have a date tonight and have some things I need to do before then."

Hadrian held out his hand, and Remy shook. "I really appreciate it, Remy."

Remy nodded again and left. Hadrian had the feeling he wasn't completely satisfied with what they'd just done. He turned and looked into the one-way mirror and saw Lucian playing with the pen on the desk.

Hadrian should have been ecstatic. He'd just arrested a man responsible for three murders. But that's not what he felt.

And Lucian wasn't a man.

He was still a boy, unable to recognize the gravity of his situation. He was seventeen, just barely, and would likely be tried as an adult. The death penalty was legal in Virginia. Lucian Cody would probably die as a result of the information he just gave Hadrian.

A heavy sigh escaped Hadrian as he went back to Sheriff Wright's office to tell her what was going on.

19

Remy stopped by Jordan's house on the way home, but no one was there. He hadn't seen her since the night before, and as silly as it sounded, he didn't like to go that long without seeing her. Every part of him told him that he'd only known her a few weeks, and that wasn't enough time to truly know a person. But when he looked at her, that's not what he felt. He felt like he'd known her his entire life.

The thought of Bethany pushed in and gave him a heavy, gray feeling. That last night he'd seen her, being hauled away and stuck in a cage to be burned like old rags... he dreamed about it almost every night. Saw her calling out to him.

"Lost in thought, brother?"

Remy looked up and realized he was sitting on the couch in their front room, staring into a fire.

"You all right?" Jerreck asked.

"I don't remember getting home. Must've got home quicker than I thought, I guess."

"And where have you been all day exactly? Out with

that Bethany twin?" He flopped onto an antique chair by the fire. "Do you even realize how obvious you are?"

"Sorry, some of us wear our hearts on our sleeve instead of hiding from the world."

"She's dead, Remy. Bethany's dead. Just because this girl looks like her… she's not Bethany."

"I know. She's nothing like Bethany. She's funny and warm and kind and actually cares about people. Bethany never cared about anybody but herself."

Jerreck took a sip of the drink in his hand. "She cared about me, and she cared about you."

Remy shook his head. "What are you doing back in town, Jerreck? There's nothing for you here."

"On the contrary. You're here."

"So you came just to antagonize me?"

He grinned. "I have thought about feasting on that little morsel of yours to see if she tastes like Bethany, too."

In a flash, Remy was at his throat. Jerreck, with a flick of his wrist, flung him back, and he rolled on the floor.

"You're weak, Remy. Weak and pathetic. And if I wanted to kill her tonight, there's nothing you could do to stop me."

"If you touch her, I will devote whatever time I have left to kill you. Even if it kills me, too."

"Something to think about. So really, where were you today?"

"Promise me, Jerreck. Promise me you won't touch her."

"Oh, relax. There are far more interesting people in

this town than Jordan Lynn." Their eyes locked. "Okay, fine. I, Jerreck Simone, promise on the scout's honor that I will not eat or kill Jordan Lynn." He raised his eyebrows. "Happy?"

Remy sat back down on the couch. If he could drink human blood, Jerreck and he would be having a different conversation. But Remy refused. Instead, he hunted rabbits and vermin in forests. Enough to survive but not enough to give him strength.

"I was at the police station," Remy said.

"Really? Do tell."

"We caught the man that killed those girls."

Jerreck didn't respond.

"You look surprised," Remy said.

"How'd you catch him?"

"He picked the girls out of a history class at the school. When Deputy Brams went to talk to him, he ran."

Jerreck shook his head. "Idiot."

"Yeah. Actually, odd you should say that, I think he might be a bit… simple. He confessed to everything with just a little prodding."

"And he's at the police station now, huh?"

Remy nodded. "For the time being. I'm sure that's gonna make this town feel a little safer. As long as you don't go out on a rampage."

Jerreck appeared lost in thought. "Have to go," he finally said, rising and heading out the door.

"Where you going?"

"Have to return a library book."

Remy looked back to the fire, playing with the medallion in his pocket. He felt incredibly tired, more so than usual. Without human blood, he was in a constant state of fatigue. He lay down on the couch and fell asleep, watching the flames licking the red brick of the fireplace.

20

Hadrian was drafting the police reports in the Lucian Cody murders. The reports were long and detailed. He wanted to make sure the prosecutor knew every single aspect of the case and precisely what Remy Simone's role had been. After all, he wouldn't be here to testify, though Building 4 might send someone else named Hadrian Brahms.

The door to his office swung open, and Deputy Clarkson was standing there. "You better watch this," she said.

He followed her out to the television. Everyone on the staff was circled around it, watching a local news broadcast.

And once again, for those of you just tuning in, another body has been found, and it does appear to be linked to both the Amanda Ronin and Rebecca Nelson cases, both killed within one month of each other. Sheriff Wright could not be reached for comment, but a spokesperson for her stated that...

"Where's the kid?" Sheriff Wright asked.

"He's sitting in a cell at the back of the station."

"And he hasn't moved?"

"I saw him five minutes ago when I took him some food."

Hadrian watched the news broadcast with disbelief. Another murder. "We need to get down there," he said. "How the hell did they hear about it before us?"

"I don't know."

Hadrian called in the forensics team, and he and Sandy raced down to the location of the body. Which they only knew by calling the news network.

Sandy was young and had her hair pulled back in a bun. She looked more like someone you'd see on a television show or working in a high-end clothing store than a cop.

"How long have you been a deputy?" Hadrian asked as he maneuvered the vehicle through the narrow streets.

"Three years, since I turned twenty-one. My dad was a cop."

"He wanted you in the family business, huh?"

"No, pretty much the opposite. He wanted me nowhere near a uniform, and I think a part of me did it just to spite him."

"Well, you're a good cop, Sandy. He's gotta be proud now."

She smiled.

The body had been found in front of an office complex for dentists' and doctors' offices. They parked at the curb. The forensics team was already there, and Hadrian stepped out and threw them a roll of yellow tape to secure the scene. A crowd had gathered, and he was worried they had already contaminated everything.

The news crew was by their van. Hadrian went over to the anchor, a middle-aged woman with strawberry hair.

"How'd you find out about this?" he said.

"Deputy, glad you could make it. Do you want an exclusive—"

"Cut the crap. How'd you hear about it?"

"Anonymous tip. They called it in."

"What'd they say?"

"Just that the body was here and there's going to be more. He had a message for you."

"For me?"

"Yeah. He said to tell Deputy Brams, 'wrong man, catch me if you can.'"

Hadrian looked back to the body. "How about next time you call it in instead of plastering it all over the news?"

"It's called freedom of the press, Deputy."

"Her parents probably saw that broadcast. How would you like to find out your daughter's dead that way?" He looked at her. "It's called being human."

He turned away from her and went to the body. The girl was young and beautiful, like the others. Her body was covered in stab wounds. Her throat was the worst —it appeared to have been ripped out entirely.

"Got an ID," one of the techs said. "Carrie Garrison. Twenty years old, lives here in town." The tech held a purse out to him.

Hadrian pulled on latex gloves before taking the purse and flipping through it. "Time of death is critical on this, Lee," he said.

"You'll need the autopsy to confirm, but, educated guess? About two to five hours ago."

Hadrian glanced around. "Keep me updated, huh?"

"Sure thing."

Hadrian turned to the crowd. "Ladies and gentlemen, we will need to ask all of you a few questions. We'll start at the end there and work our way up as quickly as we can. But please don't leave. We appreciate your patience."

He called in for a few more deputies, and the sheriff herself came down. She went on camera and gave an official statement while the body was tagged and placed inside a black body bag. Hadrian watched as it was loaded into the coroner's van and taken away.

"Sandy, can you find a ride back?"

"Sure."

He jumped into his car and took off down the road, ignoring the speed limit. He took turns so quickly, his tires squealed, and twice he ran red lights. When he arrived at the station, he ran inside to the holding cell where Lucian was lying on his back, staring at the ceiling.

Hadrian opened the cell door and went inside. "You lied to me."

"About what?"

"You couldn't have killed those girls 'cause the person who did just called us and told us where another girl is. One that was killed while you were here with me."

He smiled. "Really? So can I go now?"

Hadrian had to lean against the wall and push his anger back down inside him.

"Yes, you can go."

21

The road was dark, but with no clouds in the sky, the moon illuminated it. The asphalt seemed to sparkle from bits of glass crushed into it, and Lucian watched it twinkle as he walked home.

He had always lived in Spirit Lake. As a youth, he'd longed for life in the big cities. Manhattan, Los Angeles, Miami... someplace you could get lost in. Where whatever you did wasn't noticed by anyone else. He still longed for it, and hoped after graduation he could go to college at UCLA or NYU. Someplace he could, for once, have friends.

The only friend he could remember in his entire life was when he was twelve years old. A girl by the name of Monique. She would come over and play at his house even though he never asked her. She took him to an R movie, the first he'd ever seen. The film was about a woman who saw murders in her dreams and had to find the killer.

Once, when some boys beat up Lucian on the soccer

field at school, Monique ran over and protected him, screaming at the other boys, shoving them, threatening to get the teacher. She helped him up and walked him home.

Six months later, Monique disappeared.

Her parents tried in vain to find her for years. The police were at the school and interviewed everyone who knew her. Twice. But they never located her or found out what happened.

Lucian still saw her parents occasionally. They would invite him inside their home and feed him and tell long stories about how much Monique had liked him.

Her room was still the room of a sixth-grader, and he enjoyed going in there when the parents weren't home. He would sit on her bed and smell her clothes, the scent of dust overtaking anything else that had once been there.

A fog rolled in from the forest. He ran his hands through it, playing with the wisps that danced around his fingers. He felt cold, and the hairs on his neck stood up. He turned to see Jerreck standing behind him.

"Hello, Jerreck."

"What do you think you're doing?"

"Playing with fog."

In an instant, Jerreck was inches from him, his hand around Lucian's throat. "I checked your file at school. I read the psychologist's report. Your IQ tested at one-fifty. He considered you a genius that should be in a gifted program. You're not stupid enough to confess to everything. So I'm gonna ask you one more time, and then I'm going to rip your throat out. What do you think you're doing?"

"I knew you'd kill someone else and make it look like me. I had to do it. I had to get them off me. If they search my house, they'll find things there."

Jerreck squeezed a little tighter and then let go. "I don't like being played."

"I'm sorry. They wouldn't let me have my phone. Otherwise, I would have let you know."

Jerreck's eyes went wide and then closed to slits. "They're going to find out about you eventually. You confessed. Even with another murder, that deputy isn't just going to let this go. He probably only released you to follow you around."

"I know."

"And how do you plan to handle that?"

"I'm going to kill him."

Jerreck's face, a picture of fury, softened, and he grinned and then laughed. "It's not that often I'm surprised."

"But I can't do it like this. I need to be like you. Strong."

Jerreck didn't respond.

"Please, Jerreck. I'm ready. I've been ready my entire life. This is who I was meant to be."

Jerreck nodded. He lifted his own wrist, bit into it, and then shoved the wound toward Lucian's mouth.

"Drink."

And he did. The blood made him gag at first, but once the gag reflex calmed, it had a pleasant, almost sweet taste. Jerreck pulled away as Lucian stood there, breathing heavily, the blood running down his chin and dripping onto his clothes.

"Now what?" Lucian said.

"Now you die."

Jerreck grabbed his head and wrenched it nearly all the way around, a loud crack echoing off the nearby trees as the body collapsed onto the road.

22

Hadrian paced at the station until ten o'clock. He kept looking out the window into the darkness and then would look away and pace again.

He had been so certain that Lucian Cody was responsible for those murders. He fit the profile: loner, good enough looking to attract the girls, cold, probably with deadbeat parents or no parents at all. He had been wrong about one thing, though—he'd thought Lucian would have higher than normal intelligence.

The pacing wasn't helping relieve his nervous energy, so he stopped and sat down at the computer to try to catch up on some work from his other cases. He had a domestic violence case, a DUI he hadn't written the report for, several speeding tickets that needed to be forwarded to the prosecutor, and a possible car theft. None of them were cases he would actually follow up on, but as part of his cover he had to act like a real cop.

Forget this, he thought.

The night air was cold, and a fog had rolled in out of nowhere. He got into his cruiser and sat in the driver's seat for a long time before starting the car and heading to the Grill. That was the only place he could think to go.

The Grill wasn't packed, and he sat at the bar and ordered a beer. Remembering that his gun was still on him, he went out and secured it in his car before coming back. Next to his beer sat a Coke, and next to that, Sayer Bellamy, who smiled at him.

"Isn't it a school night?" he asked.

"There's special privileges to being eighteen."

"I wouldn't know. I never went to high school."

"Really?" she said, placing her hand underneath her chin. "Why not?"

"I tested out so I could work for the government. I figured that was what I wanted to do with my life, so why mess around?"

"You regret it now?"

He shrugged and took a sip of beer. "I guess. You know I've never been to a dance?"

"That's so sad."

"Well, what can you do? You guys seem stressed out all the time anyway, so maybe it was a blessing in disguise."

They talked a good long while, and Hadrian made sure to only sip his beer and not order another. Alcohol turned him into an idiot, so he rarely drank. If there was ever a time to justify it, though, losing a serial killer who'd confessed was it.

After a couple of hours, he gave her a ride home. He hadn't planned on it, didn't try for it, but when he walked her to her door, she kissed him softly on the lips and left him standing there, bewildered, as she went inside.

He stared at the door, his heart pounding, and then got back into his cruiser. As he was pulling away, Sayer ran back out. He rolled down his window.

"There's a dance coming up," she said. "Eighties theme. I would like you to take me to it."

"Sorry, but I really don't want to be the creepy old guy at a high school dance."

"You're not that much older than everyone there. Besides, they'll just think you're a chaperone."

He grinned. "You know, usually it's the guy that gives the first kiss and asks the girl out on a date."

"That never would have happened."

"Maybe it would have."

"Okay, so ask me."

He hesitated, but only for a moment. "Sayer Bellamy, will you please do me the honor of accompanying me to the school dance?"

"Yes," she said with a grin. "It's on Friday. Pick me up at eight."

She ran back into the house, and he watched her go.

23

Remy sat on Jordan's couch, her head resting on his shoulder. They watched one of his favorite films, *Casablanca*, which, to his amazement, Jordan had never seen.

When it was over, Jordan leaned over and kissed him.

"What'd you think?" he asked.

"Top ten favorite movies."

"It's great, isn't it? After I first saw it, I wanted to open a bar called Rick's in some Middle Eastern country."

"Well, you still can."

"I think the world's changed a bit since this came out. It's not as innocent anymore. An American bar wouldn't work over there."

"This was during a World War. I think that was a pretty messed up time, too."

He shrugged. "That was the beginning of the decline. But trust me, the world's a more dangerous place now."

Jordan's grandmother Peg walked through the front door, carrying bags of groceries. Remy went to her. "Let me help."

She hesitated, clearly surprised that someone else was there. "Thanks."

The kitchen was clean, almost sparkling, and Remy was impressed, considering two high school students lived there. Jordan's brother didn't strike him as someone who cared much about the neatness of his surroundings.

Jordan leaned against the doorframe leading into the kitchen, and the sight of her made Remy's heart jump. For a moment, he saw Bethany. A puffy blue dress, diamonds around her neck, her hair up as she made the men at a ball swoon. Like some fairytale princess from children's books.

Jerreck asked him if he had ever seen anyone more beautiful than Bethany, and Remy had to answer honestly that he hadn't. She was alluring in a way no other woman had ever been. He wanted to spend every waking moment with her, and the thought of having to do something, anything, without her there pained him.

And the worst part of it was, he knew Jerreck felt exactly the same way.

"I love her," Jerreck had confided in him.

"I know."

Remy snapped out of it when he realized Peg had asked him a question. "Sorry, what was that?"

"I said, would you like to stay for dinner?"

"Um, sure, yeah. If that's not imposing."

"Not at all. You can just take my inconsiderate grandson's spot since he never comes out of his room."

Remy smiled at Jordan, and she rolled her eyes. He pecked her on the cheek as he walked into the living room to retrieve the DVD from the player. As he did so, the television switched to the cable feed. On the screen was a reporter talking about another victim of the newly dubbed "Spirit Lake Ripper."

"Oh my gosh," Jordan said, coming up to him with her eyes on the screen. "Another girl?"

"I have to go. I'll try and be back a little later."

"Where you going?"

"I just remembered something I have to do. With my brother. I promise I'll be back later." He kissed her and was out the door before she could object.

24

Lucian felt only pain at first. A raw, aching pain that radiated throughout his body. When he woke, the pain became more centralized. His stomach… it was hunger.

Lucian sat up in his own living room. Jerreck sat on the couch, watching the news.

"They're calling you the Spirit Lake Ripper now. Once they know about you, it's usually time to move on."

"I feel like my skin's on fire."

"You're just hungry."

"Hungry for what?"

"Blood. You died and the blood brought you back. You're in transition. There's only one more step."

"What?"

"You have to be not hungry."

Lucian rose and groaned. "How can it hurt this bad?"

"Oh, that's nothing. Centuries ago, they dealt with vampires by locking them in a tomb. You would starve nearly to death, but you wouldn't die. You'd just be too weak to do anything. You'd feel the way you feel now, twenty-four hours a day, seven days a week, for hundreds of years."

"That sounds like hell."

Jerreck glanced at him and then back to the television. "I brought you a snack. She's in the kitchen."

Lucian stared at him for a long time before he walked into the kitchen, holding his gut to try to ease the pain. It felt like all his organs could come bursting out of his mouth at any second. Sweat stung his eyes, and his veins pulsated like they were expanding in his skin.

At the kitchen table sat a blonde of maybe twenty-five. Lucian grew faint. He could smell her, but not really *her*. The perfume and body wash were there, as were the shampoo and conditioner and the lotion on her hands. But he could smell something else... her blood. Staring at her neck, he saw the pounding of her pulse, and it was in sync with his own heart.

He stumbled toward her and had to lean against a chair. His eyes locked onto hers.

"Jerreck said you want to drink from me," she said. "He said I should wait here until you came in." She stood up and tilted her head to the side, exposing the soft flesh between her neck and shoulder. "Go ahead. It won't hurt."

Lucian's gums exploded in pain as his fangs descended for the first time. Blood cascaded out of his mouth as his new teeth ripped through his own sensitive flesh. But it only lasted a moment. His eyes burned, and then the only thought in his mind was taking her, drinking from her, and not stopping for as long as he could. Wrapping his arms around her, he tore into her neck.

The blood tasted like a dream. The world around him swirled, and the only thing that mattered was the blood on his tongue and the drumbeat of her heart. Maybe it was a childish reaction, but he felt closer to her than any other person he had ever met.

The drumbeat grew louder in his ears and he didn't want it to stop. The blood had slowed, so he sucked harder, tore deeper, and drank. The heart was beating furiously now, faster and faster.

In an instant, the heartbeat ceased. No more blood came. Lucian pulled out of her and watched her face. The shine in her eyes was gone. He let the body go, and it tumbled onto the floor like wet meat.

Lucian felt like he could fly. He ran out of the house so quickly it seemed like he teleported. He was outside, jumping onto people's roofs, leaping over trees, sprinting up and down the street so fast he was certain no one could see him.

Jerreck suddenly appeared in front of him. "Feels good, doesn't it?"

"I feel like I'm invincible," Lucian said, blood running down his chin.

"For all intents and purposes, you are. But a few things can still kill you. A stake through the heart and the sun are the most important ones to remember."

"But I've seen you walk in the daylight."

Jerreck held up the black medallion. "This allows me to walk in the daylight, as long as I have it with me.

You, my little vampiric nerd, don't have one. So no daylight walking for you."

Lucian shook his head. "I don't care. It was worth it."

Jerreck grinned. "That deputy is too close to catching you. I'm not telling you what to do, but... anyway. How about first you and I go get a bite to eat?"

25

Remy checked his home first. Rich was there and said he hadn't seen Jerreck. Rich was a descendant of the Simones, but because he appeared at least twenty years their senior, Remy and Jerreck told people he was their uncle. It was also good to have a human in the house. No vampire could enter a house owned by a human if they hadn't been invited in.

"Why is he back?" Rich asked.

"I don't know. Maybe just to torture me."

"Because of Bethany? That was a hundred and fifty years ago. And you guys were just kids."

"When you're a vampire, every emotion is intensified. When you're feeling an emotion, it's like there's no other feeling you're ever going to feel. Jerreck thinks I betrayed him, and he's felt that intensely for over a century. And he blames me for everything in his life. I was the one that turned him. I didn't want to be alone, and I cursed him to an eternity of hunger and death."

Remy left and checked the Grill. Sayer Bellamy was

there with another girl named Mindy, and Remy went over to their table.

"You guys seen my brother?"

Mindy had a scarf around her neck. Remy thought that unusual as it wasn't cold. He wanted to look underneath but didn't.

"Haven't seen him," Mindy said. "If you see him, have him call me."

Remy nodded. "Do the same, please."

He left the Grill and searched the town. Spirit Lake was small enough for him to cover all the high traffic areas, and he didn't see Jerreck. Which meant he didn't want to be seen.

Remy took out his cell phone and dialed Rich. "I need you to come out and help me find Jerreck. The people of this town are in danger."

The girl screamed as Lucian tore into her neck. The blood gushed so profusely it filled his cheeks.

"Her heart is strong," Jerreck said from behind them in the dark. "When you get one of those, you have to regulate the flow with your tongue. You can't just let it flood your mouth. Makes a huge mess."

The drumbeat stopped, and Lucian let the body fall. Around him, the bodies of two girls and a man lay at his feet. They were in the basement of some house. A family gathering was going on upstairs, and everyone was so drunk they hadn't even noticed their members missing.

"I'm still so hungry," Lucian said.

"You'll learn to control it. You have to. You have the potential to wipe out entire cities with your hunger. But if you do that, you'll let people on to you. And they won't stop until they find you and kill you."

"Stake through the heart?"

"That's right. Wooden. Holy water, garlic, mirrors —that's all nonsense. The sun and a good stake. That's what we have nightmares about. And something, or I should say *someones*, called Building 4."

Lucian wiped his lips with his hand. "What's that?"

"It's an ancient organization... even I don't really know anything about them. But they monitor and track creatures like... us. They have weapons we don't understand and can't protect against. If you draw too much attention to yourself, they'll come out, and they will kill you."

Lucian looked at the bodies. "Think they'll notice if one more is missing?"

Jerreck grinned. "Let's find out."

26

One in the morning and Remy couldn't sleep. He had searched the town from top to bottom and hadn't seen Jerreck anywhere. A part of him wanted to believe that Jerreck had left town. Relief washed over him when he thought that, but then the tightening anxiety came back when he realized that wouldn't happen. Jerreck was having too much fun.

Remy sipped brandy and sat on the couch in the front room. Around him hung paintings of his family. To the outside world, they were his ancestors. But that's not how he knew them. His father was looking sternly at the artist in a painting next to a bookshelf. Remy kept it there because he couldn't see it from anywhere in the room unless he deliberately looked for it. Then he thought how stupid that was, got up, and walked over to it.

The portrait was immaculately done, a real representation as good as any photograph. He took the painting down from the wall and slid it behind the bookshelf, out of view. The last time he had seen his father, his father had wanted him dead.

A deep hatred of vampires popped up from time to time. Usually followed by periods of unbelief. The culture was in a particularly long period of unbelief right now, perhaps even a permanent one. Science had killed the old gods.

The front door opened, and Jerreck walked in. He saw Remy and walked to the bar, getting some brandy of his own. "What're you doing up? Don't you have school tomorrow?" he said mockingly.

"I had to ask you something and you weren't answering my calls."

"So ask."

"I just find it a bit of a coincidence that a girl was killed while that boy was in custody. Don't you? I mean, it totally clears his name. A lot of coincidences lately."

"Yeah, weird. Hey, we got any pizza? I seriously feel like some pizza."

Remy appeared next him. "What did you do?"

"Nothing."

"You're lying."

Jerreck shrugged. "I may have helped a serial killer escape. And I may have also turned him into a vampire."

Remy's mouth nearly fell open. "Tell me you're kidding."

Jerreck took his tumbler and placed two ice cubes inside before lounging on a Louis XIV cushioned chair. "I said *may* have."

"Why would you possibly help that man kill?"

"We're killers, Remy. Don't fool yourself. You may

be drinking animal blood now, but there was a time when you would wipe out entire villages because you felt like it. You're a killer doing everything you can not to act like one."

"We have a choice, Jerreck. We don't need to be killers. But I don't get it. Why him? You know everything's more intense as a vampire. The urge he has to kill will be magnified twenty times."

"I know, weird, huh?"

"Jerreck, I'm not kidding."

"Well, I am," he said sternly. "It amused me, Remy. That's why I did it. I thought it'd be interesting to see him run around and cause havoc. And man, he is not a disappointment, I'll tell ya."

"Where is he?"

"You gonna kill him?"

"None of your business. Where is he?"

He shrugged. "Probably killing that cop."

"What cop?"

"The cop that was after him."

"Hadrian? Hadrian Brams?"

"I don't know his name. I just suggested the cop might be getting too close to catching him. Whatever conclusion he draws from that is not my responsibility."

Remy stood frozen, unsure what to say to his brother. He had thought about killing him a thousand times but had never been able to go through with it. Despite the horrible things he'd done, despite the fact that he was a monster, Jerreck was still his brother. And the only family he had left.

Remy headed out the door.
"Where you going?" Jerreck asked.
"To undo what you've done."

27

A noise woke Hadrian up. He reached under his pillow and came out with his sidearm, a Smith & Wesson .40 caliber. Sitting up in bed, he waited a few moments to see if he would hear it again. Unable to place the sound, he decided to check it out.

He crossed the bedroom and peered out into the hallway, the gun held low. Nothing. He thought it might have been a door or window opening with a creak. But it could have been the wind.

Hadrian went to the front room and checked the windows. As he turned to go back into the kitchen, he heard the noise again. It was coming from the front door.

He held up his gun. Darkness enveloped the house, and the only light came from the moon shining through the space between the blinds. He took a step forward, but then he heard the noise again and stopped.

Hadrian quickly stepped to the side of the door. He listened for anything—a voice, footsteps—that would let him know someone was out there. But he could only hear a breeze through the leaves.

As slowly as possible, he unlocked the door. The top lock first, then the bottom. Taking a deep breath, he swung open the door, holding his sidearm in front of him.

Sandy Clarkson yelped.

"Sandy, what the hell are you doing? I could've shot you!"

"I'm so sorry."

"What are you doing here?"

"I was just getting off shift. I thought you might want to hang out or something, so I was looking through your windows to see if you were in. I'm sorry, this was stupid. I'll go."

"No, wait. It's fine. Next time just text me, though. I leave my phone on."

"Good to know."

He stepped back from the door. "Come in."

He turned on the lights and got two beers out of the fridge. He handed her one and then flopped next to her on the couch. He turned on Jimmy Kimmel with the sound down low.

"Rough day at the office?" he asked.

"You could say that."

"Well, try arresting a serial killer and then letting him go."

"I heard about that. Even with a confession, huh?"

"There was another murder. DA said to cut him loose. What was I supposed to do?"

She shook her head. "I don't know."

He hesitated. "I thought that he might be working with somebody."

"Really?"

"Has to be. My gut tells me he was our man. His confession was too good, too detailed. That's one of the reasons I let him out. I'm taking some time off for the next few days and following him."

"Really? Sheriff Wright let you do that?"

"She doesn't know. And I would appreciate it if she never knows."

Sandy grinned. "Of course. I get it."

A knock at the door. Hadrian took a sip of his beer. "You expecting somebody?"

She shook her head.

Hadrian went to the door and opened it, and his heart skipped a beat.

Lucian stood there, smiling. "Hello, Deputy Brams."

"What do you want?"

"I just want to talk about something. I left a few details out of my confession."

"Fine. We can go down to the station and—"

"No, this is between me and you. No cameras, no Sheriff Wright."

Hadrian sized him up. "All right. Come in."

Lucian hesitated at the door, testing the entrance by sticking his foot through. When it crossed the threshold with no problem, he smiled widely and stepped through. Hadrian shut the door behind him.

"So what is it you have to tell me?" Hadrian asked.

"This."

Lucian swiped at him with his palm, slapping Hadrian across the chest. The blow felt like a car had hit him. Hadrian flew against the wall. He hit the floor, and he wondered if his chest was caved in.

Lucian's eyes went red, and veins popped on his face. His teeth protruded from his mouth. Sandy got up and pulled out her weapon.

"No, Sandy! No!"

Lucian turned to her and, in a blur, knocked the gun away. He grabbed her by the back of the neck and twisted, exposing the jugular vein. He bit into it and blood sprayed over Hadrian's ceiling and walls.

"No!" Hadrian jumped to his feet and ran at him. Lucian tapped him as if he were a fly and sent him onto his back again.

Sandy was groaning, and then she wasn't. Lucian held her up like a puppet. Her eyes were glossy.

"I'm Sandy," he said in a mocking voice, "and I love Deputy Brams. Unfortunately, he got me killed." He threw the body across the room, shattering the television. "And now you, Deputy Brams. I'm going to make it nice and painful. I'm going to break open your bones and drink your marrow."

He grabbed Hadrian by the throat and lifted him into the air. Lucian bared his teeth like a dog about to attack. Hadrian screamed, but Lucian crushed his throat and then he could no longer breathe.

A flash of movement and Lucian slammed into the wall. He appeared dazed, caught off guard. Lucian lifted himself up, and Hadrian saw his eyes widen as he took in who was standing over Hadrian.

Remy stepped in front of Hadrian. "I'm older and

stronger."

Lucian rushed at him. Remy grabbed him by his chest and belt and flung him over his head. Lucian crashed through the front door. Rising, he snarled like an animal and was gone.

Hadrian felt himself going out, Remy kneeling beside him.

28

Hadrian awoke in a strange place. The room looked like it was out of the Victorian era, complete with creepy paintings and a chandelier. It was still dark outside, and he couldn't see much. Two candles by the door dimly lit a figure sitting in a chair.

Hadrian felt insane. What he had seen in this life… was too much. Monsters more horrifying than anything from nightmares, things that slithered in the night inside of you, spirits that clung to places after their bodies were long dead. How much could a human mind take?

His entire life had led him to that moment. He'd chosen his career because he'd been promised adventure. He'd skipped his childhood, skipped the best years of his life, and given himself over to an organization he knew little about. Only now did he realize what a waste that had been. He just wanted it to be over. He rose and walked to the balcony. When he opened the doors, the breeze wafted over him. He stepped outside and looked down over the railing.

There'd be no more cases, no more pale broken bodies haunting his dreams. No more parents crying when he told them the grim news. No more beasts growling in the night, no more ghosts hovering over his bed. No more.

"How do you feel?" Remy Simone asked.

"My throat," Hadrian rasped.

"It's healed."

"How?"

Remy came to stand beside him. His eyes shimmered in the dark like a wolf's. "Because I gave you some of my blood. You took quite a beating from that kid."

"So he's like you now?"

Remy nodded. "In some ways. But not in others. We're not all like that. He was just turned into a vampire. Whatever you have inside you is intensified when you turn. He has nothing but bloodlust and rage."

"Sandy?"

Remy shook his head.

Hadrian tried to get up over the railing, but Remy held him down with preternatural strength. Like a statue come to life.

"You don't want to die," Remy said.

"Yes, I do. My whole life has been a waste. And Sandy's dead because of me. No one else is going to die because of me."

"It had nothing to do with you. He's a monster. If it wasn't Sandy, it would have been someone else. Please, come inside. Your emotions are just heightened now because of the blood. It'll pass."

Hadrian waited a long while, and then followed Remy in. They both sat in recliners that looked a hundred years too old.

"Then he has to die," Hadrian said. "I have to at least do that."

"You can't beat him."

"I have to."

"You can't. You saw how fast he was, how strong."

Hadrian leaned forward. "Are you telling me your kind is invincible?"

"No, not invincible. The sun and a stake through our hearts can kill us. But not much else."

"Then give me a stake."

"You have to get close enough to use it. And he's too fast for you."

Remy leaned back in his chair. Hadrian walked over to him and then knelt down. He stared into those eyes that reflected the darkness like a green sun. "Then make me one, too," he whispered.

"You don't want this. It's not a blessing, Hadrian. It's a curse."

"I have to stop him. If what you're saying is true, he's almost invincible and insane. He'll kill unimpeded. I won't let that happen because of me. Please, Remy. If you don't, I'm going after him anyway, and I'll die."

Remy sighed. "It's an eternity of hunger and almost nothing else. There's moments of joy, moments you couldn't have dreamed of as a human, but they're just moments. And then the hunger comes back."

"I don't care."

"You will care."

"Give this to me, Remy. I need to stop him."

"Why don't you let me handle this?"

Jerreck walked into the room. "I don't think so."

Remy rose and stood in front of Hadrian, protecting him. "What do you want, Jerreck?"

"You're not hurting my little toy. But the cop... now that would be an interesting little showdown, wouldn't it? Kind of decides which one of us makes the better vampire."

"This isn't a game," Remy said. "He's out there right now, killing."

"Oh, I know. Who do you think showed him how?" Jerreck looked at Hadrian and then back to Remy. "I'm afraid without human blood, he's probably stronger than you. I wouldn't risk it. Unless, of course, you'd like a little snack before going out."

Remy was lost in thought a moment.

"All right," Remy said, turning to Hadrian. "I'll turn you."

29

Kimo's Bar was packed. Perhaps forty people were there, drunk and flirting and playing pool or darts. Other than Antonio's Bar, it was the only place in the city where people could buy liquor. The city council, in an attempt to stomp out DUIs, had only granted two liquor licenses for the entire city.

Lucian walked in and went to the bar. Jerreck had told him he could drink and that alcohol actually tasted better as a vampire.

"Tequila," he said, looking the bartender in the eyes.

The bartender brought him out a bottle and poured a shot for him without even questioning his age. Lucian lifted the glass, taking a moment to enjoy the sparkling fluid and amazed that his eyes could pick up the microscopic bubbles.

He drank, and it stung pleasantly all the way down.

"Another, and a beer. Heineken."

As Lucian drank, a brunette in thigh-high leather

boots sauntered over and asked for four shots.

"You're probably the most beautiful one here," Lucian said.

The girl barely considered him. She gave him an obligatory smile and turned away from him.

"No, I was wrong. You're definitely the most beautiful one here."

The girl retrieved her shots and walked away. Lucian took a sip of his beer and followed her back to her table. She was sitting with another equally attractive girl and two beefy guys with arms that bulged in their short sleeves. They stared at Lucian in disgust as they looked over his skinny frame.

"I believe I would like a drink with the ladies," Lucian said, gazing into the first girl's eyes.

"Gross," she said.

Compulsion was something Jerreck had barely touched on. Jerreck believed it just came naturally to vampires, so there was no need to teach it. But it didn't come naturally, and Lucian had yet to make it work.

One of the men rose, towering above the five-foot-seven Lucian.

"I think you need to get outta here."

Lucian smiled. "I feel like getting thrown out tonight. You think you can oblige me?"

The stranger grabbed him by the collar and started dragging him out of the bar. Lucian flung the stranger back, and the man careened across the bar.

The other stranger grabbed for Lucian's neck, but Lucian brushed him aside. He fell to the floor and then came up cursing, his face twisted in anger.

Lucian smirked, lifted his hands up into the air, and slammed his fists into the stranger's ribs. Blood spewed out of him. Lucian smashed the stranger's head down into the table, shattering his teeth, before he tossed him aside.

Another man ran at him with a pool cue, and it so amused Lucian that he almost didn't want to fight. He grabbed the cue with one hand. The man tried to kick his groin. Lucian let him, and the man groaned as if he'd hurt his foot. Lucian grabbed him by the collar and flung him out a window twenty feet behind him.

One more man, a guy in a biker jacket, ran at him with a broken bottle. Lucian waited patiently for him to get close enough and then gazed into his eyes.

"You want to stab yourself in the neck," Lucian said.

The biker fought it, grunting as he tried to pull his hand away. Slowly, he turned the bottle on himself.

The people in the bar screamed as the biker tore out his own throat.

Lucian sat down at the table with the two girls. They were trembling. One of them smelled like cigarettes, and it made him ill. But the other smelled like oranges.

"I wouldn't try to run," he said. He lifted a beer bottle into the air. "To tonight and all its possibilities."

30

Hadrian watched as Remy bit into his own wrist. Blood, black and shiny, poured out. He placed his wrist against Hadrian's lips.

"You had some already, but it dissipates over time. Drink."

And he did.

The blood was foul, like rotting milk that putrid meat had soaked in. But he didn't stop. Somehow, he couldn't stop. The blood rushed down his throat, and he felt Remy's pulse against his lips, his heart beginning to beat in tune to Hadrian's own.

Hadrian grabbed the wrist as Remy tried to pull away, like a suckling baby. Remy had to force him off.

Out of breath and with blood flowing down his face, Hadrian said, "What next?"

"Now you have to die. Are you ready?"

He nodded.

Remy grabbed his neck and twisted, and the last thing he heard was a snap.

Hadrian saw his mother standing over a stove. She was cooking something that smelled wonderful, and he wanted to ask her what it was. But he found he couldn't speak. So he stood next to her. She turned and went to the fridge, and as she did so, she began to dissolve.

Her skin fell off, and then her bones disintegrated. Her heart flopped out onto the floor, and she screamed.

Hadrian tried to help her, but he couldn't stop her from dissolving. His father ran in and pushed him aside. But he began to dissolve, too. Hadrian screamed and ran out of the house, expecting to be on his front lawn. But instead, he was in a city.

The city was on fire. Skeletons of buildings remained, and the skies were red, the wind whipping against him so hard it hurt. No plants were left, or people. Just a vast cityscape of destruction. Fires raged everywhere he looked. He shouted for help, for someone, anyone, to come out so he knew he wasn't alone, but no one was there.

And then he heard the most terrifying noise he'd ever heard: laughter that echoed across time.

He sat up and felt hands on him. Trying to fight them off, he saw Remy's soft eyes.

"Relax," Remy said. "You're okay. You just need to relax. Take a deep breath, that's right. Take a deep breath."

"What happened?"

"You died."

"I... saw things."

"It's just your mind clinging to life. We all see things."

"A destroyed city, and then laughter. But it was horrible laughter."

Remy looked at Jerreck, who was standing on the balcony. Jerreck shrugged.

"Come on," Remy said, helping him up. "We need to go."

"Where?"

"You need human blood to complete the transformation. If you don't get some, you'll die. Take my hand."

They went out onto the balcony. Hadrian gripped his hand tightly, and in a flash, they were gone.

31

Before Hadrian even knew what was happening, they had sprinted past the forest and into the center of the city. He saw the Grill, but it was hazy and indistinct, as though he saw it through fog. He saw people and cars, mailboxes, trees, store signs... but couldn't focus on any of them.

They stopped in a parking lot next to a jeep. A girl was walking out to her car from a clothing store, and Remy went to her. He looked her in the eyes and said, "Come back with me and don't make a sound." The girl did as she was told.

"Don't hurt her," Remy said. "You don't need much to complete it. Just a sip."

"My head is pounding," Hadrian said.

"It's your body calling for the blood. You need to drink."

He shook his head. "I don't want to."

"You need to. You'll die, Hadrian. After all this, I'll show you how to control it. How to live off animals and blood banks. But for now, you have to have fresh human blood. Nothing else will do."

Hadrian approached the girl. Her eyes were a deep blue, and he saw them more clearly than he'd ever seen anyone's eyes before. The vein in her neck called to him, made his guts tighten like a fist. The pain was so intense it nearly doubled him over. He had to place his hand on her shoulder to steady himself.

"What're you doing?" the girl said. She was frightened.

Remy looked into her eyes again. "We're not going to harm you. Don't be scared."

"I don't want to do this," Hadrian said. But the words were flat and unconvincing. As he said them, he realized he had gotten closer to the girl.

His breathing was deep, and an agony was pulsating through him that made him quiver. He couldn't hold it off much longer.

Fire tore through his gums, and he screamed as he felt something sharp in his mouth. Instinct took over. He knew what they were and what he had to do.

He bit into the girl's neck, and she squealed.

The blood was unlike anything he had ever tasted. Her blood wasn't foul, as Remy's had been. Her blood was sweet and soft on the tongue. His hands gripped her arms, and she felt like overripe fruit. He knew he could crush her without even trying. How fragile human beings were.

"That's enough," Remy said. He grabbed Hadrian and separated him from the girl. Hadrian came at her again, his belly still aching, and Remy held him back. He turned to the girl and said, "You were clawed by a cat. Wear a scarf for the next two days and don't tell anyone. Now run."

The girl sprinted away, and Remy held Hadrian by the shoulders.

"I want more."

"Not now, Hadrian. Listen to me… listen to me. You can control it. It doesn't control you. Do you understand? Calm your heartbeat. Focus on it… do you hear it? Focus on it and calm it down… that's it. You're doing it. Just keep focusing on it…"

Hadrian felt his heart slow, and the fangs in his mouth retract. The world effervesced before him as if he'd seen it frozen through dirty lenses his entire life and only now could see everything clearly and in motion.

A piercing noise hit his ears, and he turned to it as Remy did the same.

"What was that?" Hadrian said.

"Screams. But they weren't close. They were at least two or three blocks away."

"How can I hear that?"

"All of your senses are heightened."

Remy released him, and Hadrian stood on his own. Power coursed through him, as did a calm euphoria. The pounding in his head was gone, and the ache in his stomach had subsided.

"It's him, isn't it?" Hadrian asked.

"That'd be my guess."

"How do we find him?"

"We follow the screams."

32

Hadrian flew across the city like a ghost. The closest comparison he could think of was the way one moved in a dream. Nothing seemed real, but everything was far more vivid than reality.

The screams were sporadic. They'd last a few seconds and then stop and start again for much longer before suddenly being cut off. Hadrian saw a bar, and people were running from it. He glanced back to Remy, who just looked at him without saying anything.

Before entering the bar, Remy placed his hand on Hadrian's shoulder and said, "Remember, it has to be a stake through the heart." He pulled a small wooden stake from his back pocket and put it in Hadrian's hand.

Hadrian nodded and stepped inside.

The bar was dimly lit, but with his vampire eyes he could see everything. Bodies were strewn on the floor, and pieces of broken glass shimmered on the ground. Hadrian heard a groan of pain or pleasure and saw a woman in a booth. Lucian was beside her, his mouth planted firmly on her empty eye socket, his eyes closed.

He let go, and the woman collapsed onto the seat. He kicked her off onto the floor.

"Hello, Deputy. Wanna have a drink with me?"

"These are innocent people. They don't deserve this."

"Don't they? How the hell would you know?" He rose and flung the table aside.

"This is Remy. He can help you."

"You're the famous Remy, huh? I've heard a lot about you."

"Have you?" Remy said.

"Yes, I have. Jerreck has big plans for you. I have no fight with you." He looked to Hadrian. "But you, Deputy, are expendable."

Remy said, "See, that's the thing. If you have a fight with him, you have a fight with me."

Jerreck was leaning against the bar, eating some peanuts out of a bowl. "I don't think so, little brother."

"This has nothing to do with you, Jerreck."

"This has everything to do with me. He's my toy. I don't want you two killing him. I'd have to go out and find another, and I doubt I'd find one as fun in this town."

"Look at these people, Jerreck. Look what he's done."

"Honestly, Remy, is this anything compared to the things you've done?"

Hadrian glanced between the two brothers. "It's all right, Remy. This is between me and Lucian."

"See," Jerreck said. "A man of reason. We'll let them fight it out. My toy against yours. Whoever wins, that toy gets left alone."

"This isn't a game, Jerreck."

"Everything is a game."

"I'm bored," Lucian said. "I think I'll just kill him now."

He rushed forward at lightning speed. He slammed into Hadrian and flung him into a wall. The stake flew out of Hadrian's hand. Lucian was in the air in an instant and came down with a knee to Hadrian's chest. Hadrian spit up blood as the knee cracked his sternum. Lucian pounded into his face with a fist.

Hadrian grabbed Lucian's head with both hands and twisted to the side. Lucian flew off him onto the floor. Hadrian jumped up and raced around the bar, but Lucian appeared in front of him. Hadrian head-butted him and got behind him, throwing him across the bar into a table.

Lucian stood. "So they made you one, too, huh? It won't matter."

"We'll see."

Lucian grabbed a bottle and broke it. He rushed in and carved up Hadrian's chest with five quick blows. The cuts seared, and Hadrian stumbled back. Lucian dashed in for a blow to the neck. Hadrian ducked and came up with an uppercut to the jaw that sent Lucian onto his back.

Hadrian grabbed Lucian by his shirt and pants and lifted him. He smashed him into the floor like a doll before tossing him through a wall into the kitchen.

Lucian was back out in an instant with a butcher knife in his hand. Hadrian caught his wrist as the knife came down toward his face. The point was tearing into his cheek, and his arms were straining at the effort to get the blade off him.

"I've fed more," Lucian said, pushing the tip of the knife farther into his cheek, his eyes blazing red. "I'm stronger."

The blade went inside Hadrian's cheek, scraping the bone. Hadrian pushed with everything he had, but the blade wouldn't come out. He glanced to his left. A table.

Hadrian let the knife fully enter his face as he rushed in and wrapped both arms around Lucian. The blade went in up to the hilt and broke off. Hadrian only felt a slight sting, though the blade no doubt was inside his brain.

He lifted Lucian and slammed him into the table, shattering it. A leg of the table splintered next to his feet. He lifted the splintered leg over his head and swooped down with both arms. Lucian grabbed his wrists, and Hadrian had to put his full weight behind it.

The makeshift stake entered Lucian's chest, and he screamed. He struggled like an animal caught in a trap. Hadrian pressed down as far as he could and felt the tip of the stake break on the floor behind Lucian's body.

Lucian's eyes blazed with fury, but his skin turned gray and wrinkled. Thick, ropey veins appeared on his face, and the fire in his eyes faded. Hadrian couldn't feel the vampire's heartbeat. A final, horrific scream escaped him before he went silent.

He stood up, blood pouring from the wound in his cheek. He tore the blade out.

Jerreck slowly clapped and said, "Bravo." In a flash, he had Hadrian up in the air by his throat, crushing it as easily as a bug. "But I'm not really one to keep my word."

"If you do it," Remy said, "we're no longer brothers."

"We're barely brothers now."

"I mean it, Jerreck. I'll be done with you forever."

Jerreck hesitated, smiled, and shrugged. "Maybe some other time. We've got eternity, after all."

Hadrian hit the floor. He felt hands on him and saw Remy's soft eyes before him as he helped Hadrian up and out of the bar.

33

The dance was packed, and Sayer mingled for some time. Several boys hit on her. They were always hitting on her, but she ignored them. They were all the same. Once they saw her intelligence, they ran scared. Something about a woman smarter than them sent most boys to the hills.

She was dressed as Tina Turner and danced with a Michael Jackson and a Ronald Reagan before getting some punch and deciding she needed a minute to herself.

She glanced around the dance several times for the person who was supposed to bring her. He hadn't picked her up and wasn't answering his phone.

Jordan was there with Remy, and they were joking around by the punch bowl. Remy gave Sayer an eerie feeling, and she couldn't quite place it. When she tried to put it into words, the only thing that came to her was that death followed him wherever he went. She hoped Jordan knew what she was doing.

Sayer left the gym and walked down the hallway

out to the front of the school. She sat on the steps, leaned back on her hands, and looked up to the moon.

Dateless again, she thought. *Way to go, Sadie.*

"Hi."

She gasped when she saw the figure standing beside her.

Hadrian was dressed in jeans and a jacket, his hair tousled. Somehow he appeared more relaxed than she'd ever seen him.

"Hey, where were you? I waited—"

"I know, and I'm sorry. More than you'll ever know." He sat down next to her on the steps. "You can't see the sky like this in Los Angeles. There's too much light pollution. It really is magnificent though, isn't it? All this heavenly glory above us and we worry about all these ridiculous things back here on our little rock."

Her brow furrowed. "Are you okay? You look different."

"Honestly, as strange as it is, I've never felt better in my life." He held her gaze. "I'm sorry I wasn't there for you. Please believe me that there was nothing in the world I would rather have done than come to this dance with you."

She smiled. "It's not too late. There's a few songs left."

"I can't, I'm sorry. I'm leaving, and I don't think I'll be coming back to Spirit Lake."

"Where you going?"

"Not sure actually. Just going to wander around for a while, I think. I've always wanted to visit Australia."

"Hadrian, what happened? Something's changed, I

can feel it. What's going on?"

He kissed her softly, his hand gently brushing aside her hair. When he pulled away, he grinned. "I hope you find what you're looking for, Sayer Bellamy." He stood.

"Am I ever going to see you again?"

"Who knows? Eternity's a long time."

He walked away. Sayer watched him go, wondering what he had been talking about. Then the doors behind her opened, and Remy Simone came out. "You okay?"

"Hadrian just left."

"I know."

"How do you know?"

"He told me he was going."

Sayer rose. "Remy, what happened?"

"I think Spirit Lake got to him. He's not the same person he was when he came here."

She shrugged. "This town can do that to people, I guess."

He grinned. "You have no idea."